Verryn's Call

Laura Harvey

The Oracle Press

The Oracle Press
P.O. Box 121 Montville Qld 4560 Australia

National Library of Australia

ISBN 1 876494 25 5

Disclaimer. This book is a work of fiction. Names, characters, places and incidents are the products of the author's
imagination or are used fictitiously. Any resemblance to
actual events or localities or persons living or dead, is
entirely coincidental.

Printed by Watson Ferguson & Co., Moorooka, Qld. 4105

This book is dedicated to my darling granddaughter
KIARA
May you grow up to be a woman of substance.

This is a story about two men at opposite
ends of the scale - Light and Evil.
Verryn loved one of them passionately,
the other one hated her
with equal passion.

If this book helps only one woman,
whether she is South African or from
any other country in the world, to overcome
the suffering and trauma inflicted by a
spiteful, vindictive man, husband or
lover, then I have fulfilled one of
my many tasks on this earth.

Prologue

Fear has a face, it is yours.
Pain, anguish and despair,
These are the scars of fear
Etched deep in my soul.

Fear buried my heart,
Made my mind retreat to secret places.
My soul bleed and flee into darkness.

You, Trevor, created and breathed fear into my life.
You relentlessly pursued me.
Controlled my every intake of breath.
You destroyed my days, minutes, hours,
My life, my very existence.

I limped through each day with fear as my crutch.
Fear – to keep moving.
Hoping distance and time would offer protection.

When would you run out of revenge
And ideas of vengeance?
When would your Maker say "Enough?"
When would you tire and rest from the chase?

I came upon an Ancient Native of Australia.
I stood gazing at him – he spoke softly.
Called me aside and quietly said,

"I take your fear in my hands and paint it here."
He drew your face in the red earth.
He wrote your name.
He spelled it wrong but he got it right.
He took my face in his dry hands and made me sit
Whilst he painted my fear on a piece of wood.

He said this would erase your hatred,
Every pain you have ever inflicted on your fellow man,
Including yourself.
He sent a message across his desert miles
With Ancestral Spirits
Called on the Universe to cloud your actions.

He said you would feel, touch, sense and smell,
The havoc and wreckage of lives touched by you.
He said you would do harm no more.
He said your power would go underground
Where it belongs.

Acknowledgements

My deepest thanks go to the following people. Without their help and support I would not have written this book.

To Samantha, Vanessa and Kyle – you are every mother's dream come true. You have made my life worthwhile and whole. I love you with all my heart.

To Lance and Adrian – two strong South African men – partners to my two elder girls.

To John, for giving me confidence and putting up with all my moods during the outpourings of this story. I love you.

To Julie, my dearest, darling friend in South Africa. Jewels, I could not find words to describe how awesome you are in spirit.

To my girlfriends in Johannesburg, Kay, Karyne, Shirley, Joy, Val and all the others. I will never forget your love and kindness given so unconditionally throughout my darkest days. I will also never forget the fun times we had.

To Helena, my beloved friend from Cape Town. Thank you for all the White Light. God Bless you, Skattie. You are so very special.

To Kathy, my sister and her little family. Thanks for all those warm and loving e-mails. I love you guys.

To my Aussie friends, Liz, Vivienne, Marnie, Hilary, Gail and all my other new but ever so special friends. Thanks for the encouragement and support.

To Neville, for waking me up to the beauty of life in this wonderful country, Australia.

To my editor, Brian Priest.

To all the people involved in the production of this book.

Lastly, but not least – thank you Australia for giving me and my family an opportunity to live!

Contents

CHAPTER ONE

The board meeting

A s I pulled into the parking area in front of the imposing entrance to Argyle Engineering, I had a quick look in the rear-view mirror. I noted how stressed I looked. It was a hot Highveld day, the steamy summer of '93. I had already held two business meetings and had skipped lunch. Feeling tired, having a bad hair day, I rushed past the receptionist and ran up the short flight of stairs to the boardroom. Fortunately, for me, the meeting had been delayed and the six businessmen seated at the heavy wood table were making small talk.

After cursory greetings I took a seat at the end of the table. The boardroom table was solid Kiaat and I ran my hand over the carved leg. I felt a rush of appreciation and affection for the African people who had painstakingly carved the figures of their ancestors and beloved animals into the beautiful, honey-coloured wood.

When I entered the room, all eyes turned my way. As they continued with their subdued conversations, I was aware of surreptitious glances cast in my direction by more than one of the men. Their interest was borne out of deep curiosity. They knew I was there to represent my husband, Trevor Grant, a powerful and influential businessman. Trevor owned shares in this business. He was demanding a withdrawal of his equity. I was there to negotiate on his behalf, as he was too busy to attend.

I had previously met the owner of Argyle Engineering, Michael Brent, at a social function. I had not spoken to him or his wife Linda for more than a few minutes. I knew that his wife was rumoured to have a drinking problem but there were always rumours in our village.

When Michael Brent entered from the inner leading door to his office, a hush fell upon the boardroom. A soft shuffling of papers and heads turned attentively towards the Chairman made me instantly aware of the personal dynamism of this man. He took his seat at the head of the table. I remember vividly how the huge oil painting of an African bush landscape hanging on the wall behind him seemed to frame him, making his presence even more imposing. Later, when I grew to know his passion for the African bush, the animals, the African people and birds, I understood why that sight of him at the boardroom table created such an indelible memory in my mind.

Michael opened the meeting and welcomed the delegates. He read through the agenda and asked whether there were any further items to be added. It was interesting to note that no one added anything to the agenda. He informed the meeting of the reason for my presence.

"Verryn Grant is here to represent Trevor Grant. We will table his request for the withdrawal of equity."

There could not have been any doubt in any one's mind that Michael considered me fully capable of standing in for my husband and that my contribution was a valued one. If there had been any chauvinistic attitudes carefully concealed by any one of the attendees, this put them to the test.

The meeting lasted for two hours. By this time I had no lipstick left. I was even more stressed by the arduous debate, which had resulted in various other options for consideration. The other shareholders did not want to raise the cash to meet Trevor's demands. They wanted him to convert his shareholding to a satellite company instead. I realised that I would have to return home to my husband without any real decision, and he would be furious.

When Michael called the meeting over I let out a sigh, and with a quizzical look on his face, he asked me if I would step into his office for a brief discussion.

As he walked to the bar fridge to get the mineral water I had requested, I noticed the quality of his suit and the expensive Italian leather shoes. We seated ourselves in the pause area of his office and I thankfully sank back into the luxurious navy leather chair. The office was like no other one I had ever seen, heavy wooden carved desk with matching chairs, magnificent paintings of wildlife, bronze statues and wooden carvings. They were all African in origin and originals. An aura of power and good taste mingling with the awesome presence of this man, I sensed his persona but also felt, deep down that something was missing.

His dark, brooding eyes camouflaged by long sweeping lashes seemed to bore into one's soul. His thick brown hair was complimented by a moustache. The moustache made him look a bit surly but I could not help noticing the perfect teeth when he smiled. His voice cut into my secret appraisal.

"Verryn, how do you feel about the counter proposal?"

"I feel comfortable but don't think Trevor is going to accept. He wants to get rid of as many assets as he can so that we can make the move to Australia."

Trying hard to remain calm and collected and to retain the business image that I projected to the outside world I was flustered by this man's penetrating gaze.

I was very much aware of how creased my linen suit was; I was hoping that he had not noticed. For some reason this man had a very disconcerting effect on me.

"Surely he will acknowledge that the counter proposal has merit. Especially since we are opening a branch in Perth?"

For an hour we discussed the various options. Looking at

my watch I realised how late it was getting. Trevor would be waiting for a report on the meeting. Gathering my briefcase and handbag I became aware of Michael staring at me and felt my face flush.

"Thanks for the drink, I am sure Trevor will contact you tomorrow some time."

I almost sprinted down the short flight of stairs but he kept good pace with me.

"Are you happy with your 740?" He was touching my car's bonnet; I noticed the shape of his hand, long slender fingers, and immaculate nails.

Our identical vehicles were the only two in the car park. His was dark blue, mine was metallic gold.

"I love my car, the only problem is that the threat of hijacking is escalating."

"I'm selling mine, I've ordered a Toyota Land Cruiser. The BMW is not rugged enough for the game farm."

He suddenly changed the subject to the setting sun. I turned to look towards the Johannesburg city skyline. It was framed in gold and orange hues. The Highveld sunsets are breathtaking. I became quiet and absorbed the freshness of the evening atmosphere. I breathed in the presence of this man standing close to me.

"Have to rush, have a good evening." I started the car and tried to concentrate on reversing without taking down one of the shade-cover supports.

I drove out of the car park with the air con on full blast and sped home. I was late and Trevor's face portrayed his irritation and controlled anger. Over dinner, the discussion and argument over my failure to close the deal, distressed me to such an extent that I told Trevor I was not attending the follow up meeting to be held the next day and that he should do so himself.

I went upstairs and lay on our bed. The huge windows overlooked the tops of the tropical trees imported and planted in our magnificent garden and the darkening sky framed the picture. The vision of Michael Brent framed by that painting in his office would not leave my mind.

CHAPTER TWO

Zimbabwe

It was two months later; we were at a game lodge in Zimbabwe. We were guests of Michael and Linda Brent, and in total there were eight of us on this trip. We had flown from South Africa in the latest addition to Michael's fleet of planes – a King Air 10-seater. The contract pilot had treated us to a full on view of the magnificent Victoria Falls on the flight in.

My husband, never popular with this group of business people, had undoubtedly only been invited for purely business reasons. The rest of the group socialised fairly often and had, over the years, become friends as well as business associates. It was quite obvious that they merely humoured Trevor and were not truly interested in his brash and arrogant conversation. They had also been compromised by his sudden decision to withdraw his shareholding in Argyle Engineering and were probably apprehensive about him doing the same with shares in two other companies in the group.

We were sitting around the huge swimming pool and there was much good-humoured teasing and banter in the group as the silent but attentive African waiters carried trays of ice-cold beers and cocktails to our loungers.

I was lying to the left side of the group, a towel draped over my shoulders, partly to avoid sunburn but also to hide the ugly scar on my left arm. Michael was reclining on a lounger to the extreme right of the group and not within my line of vision.

Linda, by now onto her fifth or sixth drink, a mixture of martinis and Corona Beers, had sauntered to the shallow end of the pool, glass in hand. She was wearing a bright pink bathing suit, which enhanced the excess weight she carried. What she did next far outweighed her lack of dress sense.

Somehow, without attracting attention, Linda had put her glass down on the brick paving, slipped into the water and removed her bathing costume. She walked out of the pool stark naked, heavy breasts sagging and waving her bathing suit above her head. She walked up to Michael and threw it at his feet, stating loudly, "You make me sick!" She then sauntered across the deck in the direction of their bungalow.

The naked back view of this inebriated blond woman was shocking and unheard of in the African bush. If I had had the time to look at the other guests and the waiters, I would have seen a kaleidoscope of shock, horror and suppressed laughter. If I was not reeling from shock I may have heard loud sarcastic laughter. It was very embarrassing.

Michael ran after her with a large towel and she shrugged him off. He managed to cover her and they disappeared behind the fringe of bush. The group sat speechless and almost in a choreographed movement, reached for their drinks and took big gulps. I got up and went into the pool.

The pool, a huge oval with planters scattered in strategic places, offered solitude and comfort in the cool water. I chose a martini seat as far from the other guests as possible and sat on the concrete slab shielded by the potted palms. I did not want to hear the ensuing discussion. Other guests where twittering and looking at our group with interest and speculation. I knew that the only person who would be vulgar enough to make derogatory comment would be my husband – he took great delight in other people's humiliation. I did not want to hear his conversation.

For ages I sat in the water lost in my thoughts. When Trevor walked up to me with a smirk on his face, I got up, took my towel and excused myself. I left him standing there, mid-sentence.

Dinner that night was at 7.30 p.m. Michael and Linda had theirs in their bungalow. The rest of the group was subdued only until the levels of alcohol consumed reached the point where inhibitions were thrown to the wind and the hilarity of the afternoon's experience could be explored. Then there was much discussion. I got up and made my excuses, going to bed early to be fresh for the planned game drive at 5 a.m. the next day. Trevor remained with the group and staggered into our bungalow at 2 a.m. I pretended I was fast asleep.

The next morning we left for our game drive and bush picnic. We travelled in two open Land Rovers driven by experienced game wardens and accompanied by an armed guard riding shotgun on a metal-crafted seat protruding from the left front of the lead vehicle.

Michael and Linda behaved in their normal, hospitable manner and she seemed to make a concerted effort to curtail her drinking, sticking to mineral water for most of the day. Michael was very quiet and seemed preoccupied. We saw very little game as the bush was extremely dry and in the heat of the day the animals sheltered in the dense shrub, too inaccessible for the vehicles. In the early part of the morning we had seen a rhino with her calf and a wild dog, which was a rare sighting as these animals are almost extinct.

We all agreed on the urgent need to dive into the pool and relax with a refreshing drink when we returned to base. Linda excused herself saying she had a headache.

I sat in the cool water watching the sun go down over the Koppies in the distance. Lost in my own thoughts and once again shielded from the rest of the group by my favourite position with the potted palms, I was taken aback when Michael swam up to my seat and pulled himself out of the water. As I reached for my towel lying on the bricks close by he took it out of my hands and threw it out of reach. It was a normal reaction for me to cover the scar on my arm when people came close to me. Now he would see it! I slid into the water until it covered my shoulders and he followed. Taking my left arm in his hands under the water he looked deep into my eyes.

"Don't always cover your arm. I have seen your scar, don't try and cover it."

As he held my arm, gently massaging the scar with one hand, I could not stop the tears from streaming from my eyes. Why was I crying? I didn't really know. Was it because he was being so gentle about something that I have been embarrassed about for virtually my entire adult life? Or was it because of his empathy in the light of what he had suffered the previous day? I could not explain my tears.

That night in the boma under a sky spangled with millions of the brightest stars I had ever seen, I watched in silent fascination as the African dancers performed their tribal dances for the dinner guests. The contrast between these native people and the international chefs imported from Italy, Germany or wherever the lodge management chose to recruit them, was stark. Together, they combined their skills to provide a feast of true African fare. Most of the meat was being cooked over open fires and the strong aromas of exotic venison, the very best of Zimbabwean beef and delectable sauces served with the usual Moet et Chandon and vintage red wines from the best vineyards in the Cape, made this a feast for the privileged few. There were candlesticks made by African carvers that stood over two metres high and the candles were the biggest I had ever seen. The flickering of these huge candles combined with the glowing embers of the fires made one forget the cares and troubles of a very stressful life in South Africa, not very far from Zimbabwe, yet very different.

When the meal was over we gathered around the fires that had been stoked up with more logs and were roaring away the chill of the night. I watched the brilliant colours of the dancing flames and wondered whether I would ever recapture the mystery of this land.

We had submitted our applications for emigration to Australia earlier that year and the process was a long and complicated one. We had heard from the migration consultant that our application was considered successful and we were waiting to be called to the Australian Embassy in Pretoria for an interview to gain final approval. I lost myself in thoughts of Australia and wondered how happy I would be.

There was no going back on our plans. Both my elder two daughters had applied for their emigration and were making plans to leave. Kelly wanted to remain in South Africa to complete her university degree. Trevor already had two of his four children in Australia and he had already decided on the emigration aspect. We had about a year before leaving our country and had to sell most of our assets before we left.

I was miles away, remembering images and events experienced on the frequent trips made to Australia over the past couple of years and did not even notice that Trevor had left our group and joined group of German tourists.

Linda had consumed much of the Moet and had retired to bed with the ever-present headache. Michael was deep in conversation with our pilot, discussing the flight plans for our return journey the next day. I got up and walked over to where Trevor was standing with a very attractive blonde German woman. I remembered seeing her at the check-in counter when we arrived.

He was expounding as usual on the topic of his immense wealth. How he went to the Mercedes Benz factory in Stuttgart and chose his vehicle on the factory floor. He was telling her about his many luxuries, mansions, holiday homes, boats, yachts and his plans to buy a 60-foot motor launch in Australia. She was hanging on his every word and the conversation, which I had heard hundreds of times, over and over, became a drone in my ears. I decided to go back to our group and do what I like best, people watching.

I saw with absolute clarity the games that people in our social sphere played. Whether we were in South Africa, Zimbabwe, Mauritius or Seychelles, wherever it was the current 'in' place to be. I was tired of the plastic conversation and the one-upmanship. I said goodnight to as many people who were sober enough to notice my departure and walked over to the armed guard who was on duty to escort guests to their bungalows.

The guard and I walked down the rugged little path. It was very quiet, only the sounds of the nocturnal insects singing their moon music. Suddenly, we were startled by Michael coming up behind us. He cheerfully chatted to the guard, said a few words in Shangaan and they laughed together. Michael thanked the guard and dismissed him at the fork in the path where our bungalow was to the left and Michael's to the right.

We stood in the darkness, dense bush surrounding us, a myriad of stars brighter than ever. I stood there, feeling the pulse of Africa in my veins, looking at this sombre but very attractive man; I knew what was to take place.

As he took me in his arms I felt a sense of sinking backwards into the night where the closeness and pressure of the stars threatened to suffocate me. Time stopped, we held onto one another tightly, breathing in the smell of each other like animals do. I moved my face to look deep into his eyes and he bent his head to kiss me.

I lost track of place, of reality, of identity, lost in the magic of this land of ours. Far in the distance I could hear the drumbeat of a village celebrating. They were honouring their ancestors and it felt like the beat was within my body.

I clung to Michael.

A million moments later we stood staring at each other and in the quietest of voices, Michael, a man of few words, said, "We are both married to the wrong people."

With that, he turned me around and gently guided me to the door of my bungalow.

Once again putting his arms around me, we held each other – not caring whether anyone would walk up on us. My heart was pounding and I could not find words to say what was reeling through my head. He took my face in his hands, stared deeply into my eyes, kissed me softly on the lips and walked away. As quickly as it had happened, Michael's shadow disappeared into the darkness.

The next day the heat was unbearable at the bustling little airport at Victoria Falls. The lonely fan turning lopsidedly did nothing to alleviate the dry heat in the customs area. We were becoming extremely frustrated by the airport officials who were leisurely checking and re-checking our departure documentation. They discussed various queries amongst themselves and one of them disappeared with all the flight plans and passports, etc. We were curtly told to be patient as no one was given preference – we had not asked to be given preferential treatment.

We knew our documentation was in order but the game of playing up to the self-importance of the civil servants and bowing to their superiority was a necessary function in order not to invoke their displeasure and cause even longer delays.

An old and wizened African woman dressed in the ethnic colours of her tribe, huge wooden rings forcing her ear lobes to almost touching her shoulders, approached our group with her basket of wares. She had all sorts of beaded necklaces, bracelets, armbands, carvings and brightly coloured clay animals. Somehow she must have sensed that I would be the only one in the group who would be an easy touch and she made straight for me. As a mark of respect in African culture, eye contact is not made. With head bowed she stood before me and thrust into my hand a leather thong with a tiny carved symbol dangling from it.

In broken English she said, "You have Amantombazana, you are a Ntombi of this Land." Direct translation means, "You have daughters, you are a daughter of this Land." I dug in my purse, gave her five Rand ($1.25) and rushed after the others who were now walking towards the silver plane shimmering on the little strip of tarmac.

Takeoff was smooth and we circled the airport to take direction south. The champagne corks were already popping. I sat with the little symbol in my hand. I had no idea what it represented. I put it in my make-up bag and closed my eyes. Trevor was sleeping and sometimes snored until I nudged him. Michael sat reading his book. Linda and the rest of the party did their usual party trick of getting smashed on the very best of cognac and Moet.

CHAPTER THREE

Life goes on

There were many more board meetings, barbecues, fancy-dress parties, birthday parties and other social occasions. Michael and I behaved the way we were supposed to. We had both been brought up by very strict, morally correct parents and we respected our marital status. We also knew that the village we lived in, despite the fact that it bordered on the huge metropolis of Johannesburg, was a haven for scandalmongers and the ever so righteous. It was also too small and incestuous, not the arena for any further contact other than business meetings and normal socialising.

We never discussed what happened in Zimbabwe, we had both blocked it out of our minds.

We carried on with our hectic lives and tried to make the most of the dysfunctional marriages that we were both locked into. Whenever we met it was difficult not to maintain eye contact and we were, undoubtedly, transmitting messages to each other but the spoken word never happened. I sometimes felt that I had dreamed the whole episode.

Telephone calls, always with a business purpose, sometimes left one of us holding on at the end of a sentence, waiting for the other to make the next move.

One night, we were at a braai at a mutual friend's house. I was wearing soft beige pants with a matching top – loose and flowing. The outfit was made of a fairly flimsy material and I had brought a jacket in case it got cold. I had left it in Trevor's latest toy and it was parked quite far from the house down a circular driveway. I asked him for the car keys so that I could get my jacket.

He made a huge issue of whipping out the keys, solid gold key ring with the Porsche logo, giving me loud instructions on how to use the unique alarm system, specially designed for the newest model and enhanced for the South African market. Before he had finished his little charade, having successfully gained the rapt attention of a few 'hangers on' Michael was standing beside me. He was holding his own jacket.

He took my left arm, guided it into the sleeve of his jacket, then the other arm, turned up the collar and fastened the button – in front of everyone! I stood there speechless with embarrassment.

Michael turned away. Trevor laughed loudly, calling after him.

"Hey Mr. Smooth, are you practicing to be a gentleman?" Michael ignored him. I walked away and stood at the braai fire hugging the jacket to my body.

Two weeks after this incident I was at a charity golf competition. Michael had invited me to participate in a four ball. The other two men were members of his management team. I had only been playing golf for about three months and was still very nervous in front of experienced players.

The men were all good players, Michael was a 12 handicap. I made mistakes all the time, fluffing my balls, swinging wild, taking my eye off the ball, standing badly – you name it.

I could sense the irritation of the two men but Michael was incredibly patient and supportive, showing me how to stand and correcting my grip. When he stood close and moved my hands to a better position, I found myself holding my breath and trying not to lose concentration. My game deteriorated and I decided to withdraw but to walk the rest of the course with the players.

Standing back and watching Michael teeing off was fascinating. I will never forget the way he looked that day. He was dressed in dark grey trousers, light grey golf shirt and wearing a Ping golf cap. His caddie, Alpheus, was wearing identical clothing supplied by Michael.

As he moved into the swing his body became feline and fluid and the look of single-minded concentration on his face showed the determination and skill he was known for. I could not get enough of watching this man. My emotions were in turmoil. Could I be falling in love with him?

CHAPTER FOUR

Trevor

I had become accustomed to my loveless marriage with Trevor. We had been married for eight years. He was my second husband and I was his fourth wife. After my husband died, I had been alone for many years and had not wanted to get married again. I had a successful business and adored my three daughters. My social circle kept me busy, I had a few very loyal girlfriends and enjoyed a comfortable lifestyle.

Trevor entered my life and swept me off my feet. Fifteen years older than I, he exuded charm and confidence. He wined and dined me and showered me with flowers and gifts. He was a wealthy and powerful man and many people were in awe of him. I admired his outward image of being a successful businessman and could not understand why so many people seemed to dislike him intensely. I decided that the openly disrespectful and contemptuous people were merely jealous of his wealth and standing.

He had been a late starter, had only gone into his own business in his early forties and had enjoyed a meteoric rise to riches. He came from a very poor and uncultured background and had not been educated. He often used to boast that he had never read a book from beginning to end in his entire life.

I was intrigued by Trevor Grant. He was very protective of me and would not allow me to drive to the petrol station to fill up my car, as he feared that I would get hijacked. He insisted on doing all the 'man's work' in my life and subtly took control. He started visiting my businesses and sent his technicians in to re-evaluate my stock levels and drafted training programs for my staff.

Slowly but surely, Trevor made me dependant on him and I started enjoying the feeling of being 'looked after'.

When I look back now I can see the common tactics he used. He used them on every person who entered his life, whether it was personal or business. He was the ultimate control freak. Once he had you locked into his 'system' he called the shots and manipulated and you became a puppet.

After two years of courtship we got married in a tiny Chapel in the village where we lived. We were well known in the village and our marriage sparked off much controversy. There were people who said I was a 'gold digger' and that I had married him for his money. There were others who knew more about me and knew that I had enough financial security in my own right. They knew that I did not need a rich husband. Trevor's children, however, stuck to the 'Gold digger' opinion and made my life a misery from day one.

They were blatantly rude and obnoxious and their attitude to their father was disgusting. They openly spoke about his future death and their pending inheritances, treating him with total disrespect and animosity. I could never understand why his children hated him so much. Years later, when I heard parts of the history, I realised why this family was so dysfunctional. Most people known to Trevor knew about his dislike of his two sons, whom he spoke badly about, and that he barely tolerated his two daughters. He had no family loyalty whatsoever.

At this time in my life I was oblivious to the politics and the deep rooted hatreds raging in his family. I enjoyed his attention and felt that he could take over the reins and I could be a 'real woman'. I often joked with my girlfriends who had 'normal husbands and lead normal lives' – saying that I wanted to be a protected and kept woman and not the driving force in my family. I had worked all my adult years and never had the pleasure of raising my babies. My first husband, Rowan, was killed in a car accident when the children were very young. I was left to run our fairly large advertising business.

Rowan and I had started the business and had worked day and night to build it. Our combined business skills and determination to succeed resulted in a highly profitable and well respected business.

I had grown up in a strong business environment. Both my parents had been excellent business people and had owned some prosperous businesses in the motor industry.

I saw in Trevor a good businessman, a leader, a financially secure man, a protector and most importantly, I thought he would never be unfaithful. He came across as being totally devoted and I basked in his love and attention. My late husband had subjected me to the humiliation of his dalliances with a couple of members of our staff and I had never really shaken off the fear of being cheated on.

This fear had prevented me from entering into relationships in the period between Rowan's death and marrying Trevor. The men I had dated in that period had all fallen short of my expectations. They were too emotional, too insecure, too vain, lacking in business sense, not intelligent enough and none of them passed the 'loyalty' test.

Enter Trevor, much older, wiser, protective and highly unlikely to want to mess up another marriage. He was exactly what I wanted. I had become very reclusive and had started to feel the loneliness of a woman whose children were making their own lives and the looming of the 'empty nest syndrome' made me vulnerable. Trevor Grant had decided that he wanted me to be his wife and he was an expert at the game.

I should have heeded the subtle warnings given by people

and the vague uneasiness I felt deep in my stomach – especially the day when Trevor said to me, "I always get what I want. I never give up and I want you as my wife."

After our marriage we combined our businesses – they were in related industries in the engineering sector. Trevor insisted that I take up the role of director and we split the company in half as far as responsibilities were concerned. He looked after production and finance, I looked after marketing, sales, warehousing and new projects.

After spending one month in the business I was shocked at the new image of Trevor I was presented with. I was stunned at the way he spoke to people and how he raged through each working day. He fired a manager without so much as an enquiry into what the poor man had supposedly done wrong.

Later on in the marriage I could only term his behaviour as brutish and callous. Yet at this stage I made excuses for his behaviour. He had too much pressure, he was a workaholic. You don't succeed in business unless you're tough, etc., etc. I had a million reasons for this change of persona and would not accept that I had made a dreadful mistake. I was going to work this one out and our marriage was going to be happy.

Perhaps I should describe Trevor. He was about 170 cm., stocky in build with rough, blunt features and a full head of ginger hair. Trevor never smiled; one never saw his teeth. He had thin lips and a constant downturn to his mouth. The way I describe him sounds so awful and nasty but after becoming another one of his possessions and then a victim, I cannot find anything good to say about him.

After six months in the business I accepted that the Trevor who courted me so lavishly and with so much affection was a figment of the past, a shadow. I now had to deal with the real man.

He had an aggressive, autocratic attitude and always

demanded his own way. He had no regard for social graces. He was a hard taskmaster, treated his staff with utter contempt and was nicknamed 'Hagar the Horrible' by many of them. He was an utter racist and had no regard for the feelings of any one of the three hundred black people employed in our factories.

I started withdrawing from too much contact with him during each business day and immersed myself in the job of building up the business. It was spiralling into debt and losing market share on a rapid scale. He had been too busy travelling the world with an assortment of lady friends, wives and other companions to notice that his business was floundering. He adopted a haughty attitude in the market place; completely unaware that his business had been declining for the past five years and the rot had set in.

He employed a team of managers who hated him. They were totally unproductive and merely put on a show of working. The atmosphere prevailing throughout the business was that "The old man has pots of money and no one really has to work. He will keep putting money in to keep it sailing." I could see the writing on the wall and tried to alert him to the pitfalls and the very real threat of bankruptcy. He rejected my opinions and ideas and obtained a R3 million ($750,000) overdraft for the company.

CHAPTER FIVE

Working with the man

It took me six months to recruit a sales team, train them and allocate their respective areas. On the team I had seven men, two of them were very proactive and innovative thinkers. They were the leaders of the pack and the others, all with special skills of their own, allowed these two to do the creative thinking.

Our business, once a leading manufacturer of automotive components, had to regain the respect and acceptance of the motor industry.

We had worked long hours on drafting a new business plan. With much excitement one afternoon I walked into Trevor's office, the inner sanctum where the managing director of this huge business spent his day playing solitaire on his computer. The office was ornately decorated in bright red and black with leather chairs that were so glossy they looked like plastic. A black enamelled coffee table took centre stage in the pause area.

No rough wood or genuine pieces of art for this man. He was the king of his domain and wanted people to know what his wealth stood for – plastic and expensive.

He looked up from his computer and stared vacantly. "Trevor, the marketing team and I have completed our business plan for the new financial year. We would like to present it to the management team as soon as possible."

"Well, if you really want to do that, make it Friday at 4 p.m."

"That doesn't leave us much time to do a proper presentation. Could we make it earlier – the guys would like to go home early on a Friday."

He ignored me and started playing with the keyboard. Gritting my teeth I obeyed, "Okay, we'll do it at four o'clock." I went downstairs and asked my secretary, Merryl, to type the agenda and circulate it to the managers.

At four o'clock that Friday we assembled in the boardroom. My team had all waived my apologies for the late call on the meeting but the senior managers were looking glum and disinterested. Trevor kept us waiting for 20 minutes and when he eventually walked in he made no apologies or excuses, he merely glanced around the table to see whether anyone had dared to be absent.

Taking his place at the head of the glossy black boardroom table he launched into the format of our normal management meetings. He completely ignored the fact that this meeting had been called for the presentation of the sales and marketing plan. As was customary, he recounted all the negatives of the preceding week and went around the table forcing certain the unlucky staff members to answer publicly for their shortcomings.

To watch these men squirming and making lame excuses for things beyond their control was frustrating and degrading – they had no authority but they were held accountable. Trevor ruled his side of the business in an autocratic way and made all the decisions. If things went wrong, which they often did, he blamed his managers.

By the time he got to the end of his usual tirade he was bored and irritable and it was obvious that he wanted to close the meeting.

"Trevor, can we please make our presentation now? It is getting quite late." I realised I was running out of time and had to run the risk of his rudeness.

Emphasised with an abrupt motion of his hand he said, "Very well, keep it brief."

By now I was feeling drained and I could see that my team were becoming unsettled.

I gave a short overview of the projections, leaving out the bulk of the facts and research and not even bothering to use the overhead slides that we had produced with much anticipation.

Closing with a positive statement on the research and design of new products and market survey results indicating the need for them I sat down and waited for the reaction.

There was a moment of silence when everyone in the room looked at Trevor, waiting for his response.

"You and your Merry Men are talking shit!" He got up and walked out.

The stunned silence was too much for me to bear. I got up, gathered my papers and followed him into his office. I threw all my presentation folders on his desk, scattering pens and papers everywhere. He was so surprised that he knocked a glass of water over and started picking up papers and mopping up.

In silent fury, with tears streaming down my face I stared at him, forcing eye contact. "I am resigning, I don't need this humiliation anymore. I cannot work with you any longer."

My team had dispersed to their office, preparing to leave the premises in silent dejection. I ran to my own office trying to avoid contact with them and started packing up my desk.

The factory manager, a soft natured person, put his head around the door, "Congratulations on an excellent plan, Verryn. When do we go ahead?" I shook my head, unable to find words and turned my back so that he could not see my tears.

Still shaking, I stormed out of the building and headed for the shelter of my car.

Driving down Kloof Road, I passed Michael's house. With

abnormally high security walls and electric fencing above the walls, great imposing metal gates and cameras swirling from side to side, it was the picture of South African home security.

I saw his car on the driveway and on impulse dialled his cell phone from my car phone. When he answered, I could not talk. He must have seen my number displayed on his cell phone because he said, "Verryn, is that you? Say hello."

"Michael, can you meet me for a drink at the Pig and Whistle. I need to talk to someone right now."

"Be there in five minutes." His phone clicked off.

I parked outside the noisy Irish pub and waited for him.

Sitting way back in one of the cubicles I told him the whole story. He ordered the second round of drinks, lit a cigarette and leaned back with that serious, dark look that I later grew to know so well.

The waitress brought our beers and Michael pushed the slices of lemon into the bottles of Corona. Leaning forward he took my left hand in his hands and started twirling my wedding band round and round.

"How would you like to work for me – I need a marketing director – you can start Monday."

"Thanks, but no thanks. Trevor would go mad, he would never allow me to work for you – you know that."

Michael seemed to freeze; abruptly he let go of my hand and sat back. It was if a shutter had come down between us – he was cold and aloof. I learned later that Michael was very prone to mood swings and I never really got to grips with this facet of his behaviour.

I felt better, having cried on someone's shoulder and decided that I should go home and face Trevor.

"Thanks, Michael. I'm going home now." I got up to go.

"Sit down Verryn, I need to talk to you."

Leaning forward, he took both my hands in his, those dark

brown eyes boring into my soul.

"I love you. More than anything or anyone. I will do anything for you." His voice faltered and he looked down.

I knew that he meant it. I loved him too.

"Leave Trevor. I'll ask Linda for a divorce. Let's go to Australia and start living. Please?"

The emotion in his voice left me trembling. This was too quick, too unexpected.

I knew all about his plans for buying an engineering business in Perth. Suddenly, the prospect of a new life in Australia seemed so exciting. Instead of existing from day to day, living with someone I barely tolerated, I could be with Michael. He would love me, hold me, talk to me, share with me. We would enjoy a life of tenderness. My imagination was running away with me and I sat back, dreaming.

Reality as it always does, slowly crept into the picture.

How could we do this? What about my three daughters? I was a married woman and had responsibilities. Michael had responsibilities. Linda had a serious drinking problem, how would she cope. The questions were reeling through my mind.

I reached for his hand across the table. "Michael, I don't know what to say. I think you know how I feel about you. What about the others?"

"We can work it all out. Just say yes... we'll take one step at a time."

I felt the fear of losing his friendship. "What if I can't do this, does it mean the end of our friendship?"

I waited, dread coursing through my veins.

Michael and I had developed a close friendship built on trust and common values. We interacted very well in the business scene and up until then had been careful about hiding our emotions. Now we had crossed another barrier and we had to face whatever the challenges were.

We decided to thrash the problems out over dinner and he called the waitress. We ordered a pub dinner each and a bottle of Chardonnay.

My cell phone rang. Trevor's voice boomed. "Where are you?"

"I'm at the Pig and Whistle, having dinner."

"What are you doing that for? The maids have prepared food for us!"

"I'm with Michael, I'll see you later."

"No you won't. I'll join you." He clicked off.

Michael smiled when I told him. He leaned back and lit another cigarette.

When Trevor strutted in I could see the aggression on his face. He looked around with his customary air of condescension and marched over when he spotted us.

Michael lifted his glass to me – a silent toast to me and to what was going to happen.

Trevor sat down, the look of displeasure intensifying. He considered this pub too 'down market' for him and refused Michael's offer of food. He lifted the wine bottle out of the ice bucket.

"This has to be the crappiest label – why don't you order decent Chardonnay!"

The waitress arrived with our food. Michael and I ignored his comment.

"Bring me a bottle of Simonsig Chardonnay." He issued an instruction, not a polite request. The young waitress gave him a scathing look and walked away to do as she had been told.

We made a bit of small talk. Then the typical bluntness.

"What's the reason for this meeting? Why are you two huddled in this dump?"

My anger surfaced. I had enough of his sarcasm, his rudeness and his never ending aggression.

I told him point blank what had transpired since I left the

office, enlarging on the offer from Michael.

"What bullshit! You will not leave our business! The answer is NO!" He was shouting and people were staring.

Michael had not spoken, his eyes had followed the conversation. He seemed withdrawn as he sipped his wine. In typical vein Trevor changed the topic and started waffling about meaningless things. The job issue, as far as he was concerned, was no longer worth discussing. Michael never uttered a word in acknowledgement of Trevor's inane comments. He stared deep into my eyes. He seemed to be looking into my soul.

Eventually he leaned forward, ignoring Trevor in mid-sentence. "What's your decision, Verryn? Are you accepting my offer?"

Trevor answered for me – barely controlled malice making his lips curl and revealing his teeth.

"No way, no way! She is NEVER going to work for you. She stays where she belongs."

Michael's voice was deadly in its quiet tone. "You are married to the worst kind of bastard. It is made worse by the fact that you have to work with him all day. He will continue to humiliate you and drag you down to his level. Do you feel that unworthy that you need to take his belittlement of your talent and efficiency? Stay where you are – my offer stands indefinitely."

He leaned back, lit a cigarette and stared at Trevor. Trevor would not maintain eye contact. He drank his glass of wine, threw money on the table and stalked out.

I grabbed my handbag and made to leave. Michael pulled me down. Cold anger making his voice icy.

"Stay here, I want to talk to you."

I had never seen such controlled anger in a human being. A pulse was beating in his temple. His dark brown eyes seemed to change colour, turning black.

He took my hands in his and started talking. What Michael told me that night, I never repeated to another person. He told me about my husband and what he stood for. He did not go into detail, merely informed me of the small fact that I was married to a gangster. My blood ran cold.

I sat there, speechless, flashes of events, places, conversations, coming in and out of my mind. So much was falling into place. How could I have been so blind? I needed time to think.

"Michael, I am going now. Walk with me to my car please." Suddenly I felt afraid. Not afraid of hijackers, there were guards in the car park. I feared something else; I could not put a finger on it.

We stood in the car park. The night was warm and crystal clear. The scene inside the pub was still rattling around in my brain and I was trying to remain calm. Michael leaned on my car, putting his head in his hands. I stood there not wanting to leave him. I wanted us to get into one of the cars and drive away forever, just the two of us. Gently he took my cars keys from my limp hand and opened my door for me. Helping me into the car, his voice was husky, "If you have any problems tonight, phone me. My cell phone will be on all night. I will come to you whatever the time is. I love you."

I drove home in a daze. How could I face Trevor knowing what I knew?

When I got home he was not there. I assumed that he had gone to the club not far away. Most of the business people in the village belonged to this private club. I knew he would seek the company of the usual hangers on who pandered to his ego.

I took my toiletries and nightclothes and moved into the guest bedroom, locking my door.

The next morning I got up very early and left the house without seeing Trevor. I went to the factory and started packing up the personal belongings in my office. Being Saturday, the only staff on duty was the factory manager and some of his labourers.

Trevor walked in to my office while I had my back turned to the door. I heard his breathing as he stood behind me. My heart stopped. Turning slowly I looked into those dull green eyes and knew without doubt that he was going to win this round. I realised that I had developed another emotion for him – fear.

"You will have a 50 per cent stake in this business as of Monday morning. No more crap about leaving. Do we understand one another clearly?"

"Trevor, I am a human being, not a possession. You cannot make me do anything against my will."

He took two steps closer to me, his lips tighter than ever. "You are a possession. MY wife. I own you."

"You own me but you don't love me!" My voice rose and he seemed taken aback.

"I do love you Verryn. You are the only woman who has ever shown me love. I do love you, in my own way."

We stood there, sentence for sentence, on and on. Me wanting to leave. Him telling me why I couldn't go.

My resolve from the night before was crumbling. The prospect of divorce was just too much to bear. I could not envisage facing my girls with this problem. Trevor would make my life unbearable. I knew it.

I went home leaving him at the factory. I lay on the bed in the guestroom and slept for the rest of the day. My body was aching with indecision.

For the remainder of the weekend Trevor treated me like a fragile doll. He fussed over me, took me to a restaurant for Sunday lunch. By the end of the weekend I had decided to try and make the marriage work. I agreed to continue working in the business.

Michael had called me twice, once on Saturday and once on Sunday when I told him about my decision to stay with Trevor. His response was blunt. "You are wasting your life. I am here for you, always. Remember that. Call me if you have any problems no matter what they are."

The only reminder of this incident was that from then onwards my team dubbed me Robyn Hood. The rest of the company affectionately referred to us as Robyn Hood and her Merry Men. Trevor never commented on this and I think the significance was lost on him.

CHAPTER SIX

Linda runs away

It was June 1994. We had socialised and partied with Michael and Linda many times during the last year. We also suffered a repeat performance of her nude bathing. This time she chose to pull the stunt at the plush Royal Palm Hotel in Mauritius. Fortunately for her topless bathing is the norm in Mauritius and one often sees women of all shapes and sizes sunning themselves on the snow-white beaches. However, topless bathing at hotel pools only seemed to appeal to the very young and very beautiful. German and Swiss tourists often paraded their jet set suntans and gave serious competition to the more sedate South African visitors. Linda did not care. She was there to humiliate Michael.

The incident in the pub was never referred to again and Michael and I carried on with our separate lives. We dedicated most of our time to our respective businesses and he was often overseas.

Linda had decided to redecorate their home and Michael gladly gave her the go ahead. He wanted her to be occupied and the decorating project would keep her busy for a while. A top interior decorator was commissioned and their home, undoubtedly one of the most palatial in the area, had a complete facelift. A huge indoor swimming pool was built to cater for Linda's predilection for nude bathing.

The pool atrium was tiled in the very best of Italian tiles and the end result was striking and almost unbelievable in its luxury. The tiling contractor, a Portuguese man by the name of Luis, had been contracted for this project. He was well known for his excellent workmanship. He was also well known for his charm.

At their 'house warming' party, with almost one hundred guests present, I was surprised to see Luis. It was very unusual for the elite circle of Bedfordview to invite tradesman to their functions. I assumed that Linda had invited him out of gratitude and he was certainly receiving the accolades for this project.

Two weeks after the party Michael came home to find a note from Linda informing him that she had left the country. She had run off to Portugal with Luis. She wrote that they were madly in love and could he divorce her as quickly as possible.

Michael went into one of his reclusive periods. He had many of those in his lifetime. He spent many weekends on his game farm, Falcon's Rest, in the Eastern Transvaal with only his loyal staff for company. This farm was one of the most exclusive in the area and bordered onto the Kruger National Park. Michael had gained permission from the park authorities to pull down the fences and the game from the National Park roamed freely throughout his property.

The only times I saw him was at board meetings and we had no telephone contact for months on end.

Towards the end of the year Michael bought himself another aeroplane. He now had three aircraft and had become an accomplished pilot of light aircraft. His largest one, the King Air we had travelled to Zimbabwe in, was out of his scope of piloting and he used to contract the best available pilots to fly it. He used his own aircraft for business travel and pleasure trips, mostly to Zambia, Namibia and Zimbabwe.

We began getting invitations to join him and the rest of his social circle for trips to the game farm. I knew why we were being invited. It was no secret that Michael's clique did not enjoy Trevor's company. They tolerated him, only just.

We would board the Cessna at Lanseria Airport and fly into Skukuza. Here, we would be welcomed by Vusi or Philemon, the two game wardens employed by Michael. They would drive us in an open Land Rover to the beautiful home set deep in the African bush.

These weekend trips were blissful. We would get up at 4.30 in the morning and climb onto the waiting Land Rovers for the early morning game viewing. We were often lucky and in one day we would get to see the 'Big Five', elephant, lion, buffalo, rhino and leopard.

At about 8.30 we would stop at a waterhole for breakfast. The warden on duty would offload the cooler boxes with delicious fruits in season and chilled champagne. He would then cook a sizzling breakfast on the portable barbecue and we would sit in the shade of a tree discussing the game we had been so privileged to see.

The sight of a magnificent pride of lion lazing in the early morning sunlight, tummies full from the previous night's hunting, was something that always evoked a sense of wonder. The little cubs used to gambol and play while the watchful lionesses kept them under constant surveillance. The king of the pride normally dozed off, only moving his tail to rid himself of the pesky flies.

Then there were the elephant herds. Such majesty and awesome power. We kept a respectful distance, watching them slowly walk across the road, their massive heads lumbering from side to side with their huge ears flapping. There was no obstacle big enough to deter them from their intended journey and feeding.

We would then drive back to the homestead and spend the afternoon at the stunning black pool, set into a wooden deck jutting from the side of the house. It provided a spectacular vista of dense bush and rolling hills, which opened up to the national park in the distance. We would sit with ice-cold Coronas and discuss the morning's viewing. I have yet to meet a South African who is not enthralled by the wild animals and bush of this country.

The colours of the African bush are unique in their intensity. Different seasons bring different colours. In one outing you could pass through many different kinds of landscapes from dense bush to the rugged and unforgiving. Here, you would see very few animals as their coats offered perfect camouflage. The beautiful leopard could be seen resting high in a tree, his kill hanging from a branch.

There were forest settings with creepers on every side where elephant herds and many different species of buck made it their domain. Cheetahs roamed flat veld country with dry, rocky outcrops. Small koppies with abundant indigenous flora. Dried up waterholes with black mud and small stagnant pools of water attracted the powerful buffalo.

Shrubs and trees cascaded to the water's edge of lush riverbeds as hippo faces surfaced now and then. In more remote areas there was the ever-present danger of the African crocodile.

We would gather on the veranda at 5.30 in the afternoon for the evening game drive. The Land Rovers were well equipped with blankets and cooler boxes. The vehicles had been fitted with powerful spotlights with long cords. Although they were mounted to the windshield, they could be lifted out of the brackets and operated by hand. The guard 'riding shotgun' would normally take the spotlight and play it from side to side spotting game in the darkness. Riding shotgun was the term used for the game warden seated on a metal chair welded to the chassis of the vehicle. The guard would sit there, his shotgun clipped into a bracket mounted on the bonnet. His main duty was to spot the game. He also instilled a sense of security, as he was also there to protect us in an emergency. Both Vusi and Philemon were experienced game trackers and they would see animals before any of us did.

In the darkness, with stars sparkling in indigo blue skies, we would sit for hours watching a night kill. Two or more agile lionesses would take down a zebra on the run and once again feed their families and hyenas would voice their delight. Their demented laughter was spine chilling.

On one of these game drives, during winter, we had colourful Sotho blankets to wrap ourselves in. I was sitting in my favourite position in the back row of the open Land Rover. This bench was elevated, higher than the front and middle rows. It was not a popular choice, as you had to keep your wits about you and duck the low-hanging branches of the thorn trees. Although the benches were upholstered, the lack of good shock absorbers was still felt! The viewing from this seat was superb and I was also at a distance from Trevor. He always chose the front passenger seat next to the driver where he could issue a never-ending stream of instructions. It was the only comfortable bucket seat. I used to smile inwardly at the polite way the African wardens used to ignore him.

Michael climbed up beside me. His friends, Hilton and Carry, were seated in the middle row. It was cold and my blanket kept slipping from around my shoulders as we bumped along the rough track. Michael leaned over to tuck the blanket around me and as he did this I looked into his eyes. I saw, without a shimmer of doubt, the longing, the love and the utter despair of this man. The reality hit me. I was being an utter fool. Why waste each precious day living with a man like Trevor when I could be held and loved by Michael, an exciting and awesome man.

Michael had a magnetism that I have never felt with any other human being. I can only equate the power of his persona to the feeling I got that night when we parked in thick bush and quietly observed a pride of lion walking in the moonlight. They wove their majesty around the African landscape. The male lion, leader of the pride, walked with feline grace and absolute confidence in his supremacy. Michael walked liked that – tall and confident. He strode purposefully and exuded strength. He had an air of culture and aloofness that made him unfathomable. He was a very rare kind of man.

That night dinner was served in the Boma. This is the name for a circular shelter made of cane and reed. It is symbolic of game farms and offers protection from wild animals. It has no roof and the cooking is usually done over open fires. A roaring log fire would always be made near the opening of the boma to deter wild animals.

Elsie, the farm cook, had excelled herself that night. We had enjoyed a venison 'potjie' and fresh vegetables. She had make a delicious milk tart for desert and the noble wine rounded off a truly delicious meal.

I sat staring into the flames of the roaring log fire. The night breeze played with the flickering candles on the roughly-hewn table at my side. I looked up at the stars and searched for the brightest one. I always use to imagine that this star was Rowan, watching over the girls and me. Silently I asked him what I should do.

As if in a whisper, my inner voice said to me, "Rather love for a brief period than never love at all." I don't know why I sensed, even then, that Michael and I would not have much time together. It must have been the ancient wisdom of the Bush Fairies preparing me for the inevitable.

I decided there and then that I would ask Trevor for a divorce at the first opportune moment.

I never got around to it. That night Trevor became ill. He was passing blood and we made a hasty return to Bedfordview.

During the following week we visited doctors and specialists. Trevor would not accept their diagnosis and decided that he would contact a physician in Germany. He had met this renowned doctor on one of his overseas trips.

We made plans to leave for Germany.

CHAPTER SEVEN

Australia becomes a reality

Trevor underwent numerous tests in Munich and was diagnosed as having a problem with his prostrate gland. It was not malignant and he was put onto heavy medication. We returned to South Africa and heard the good news that our emigration application for Australia had been granted. At the same time our business had been bought by a huge conglomerate and we had to make plans for our future.

There was too much happening in our lives. The thought of divorce was once again pushed into the recesses of my mind.

While we were in Germany Trevor had been very kind and loving to me. I began to think that there was hope for our marriage and that my feelings for Michael were nothing but infatuation. Besides, most of our children would be living in Australia. Emigration was traumatic in itself, divorce would double the strain.

In the meantime, Michael had sold his business to the largest engineering group in the country. As a condition of his sale contract he had to remain as CEO of the business for a period of three years. He had bought a business in Perth and sent one of his former employees to manage it for him.

Trevor and I left for an extended trip to Australia. We visited Perth, Sydney, Melbourne, Adelaide and Brisbane. We were unsure of where we wanted to settle. His two sons lived in Adelaide. He was not that keen on living near to them as he had a bad relationship with both of them. We also did not know whether we wanted to buy a business or retire. Trevor kept talking about buying the motor yacht he dreamed about and he started visiting the boat manufacturers.

He met up with some yachtsmen on the Gold Coast and that was it. He made the decision without consulting with me. We were going to live in Brisbane and he was going to sail the waters between Brisbane and Sydney.

I was happy with his decision as Sarah and Amber had bought a small manufacturing business in Brisbane. They were over the moon at the prospect of me being close to them and offered to sell me a share of the business. I jumped at this opportunity. I could get back into a business role, which would save me from the sailing excursions. I could not imagine anything more soul destroying than being isolated on a yacht with Trevor and his monotonous conversation. Undoubtedly, he would install a sophisticated computer system on the boat and then he could play solitaire all the way.

We spent the last two weeks of our trip in Brisbane. The loving attitude portrayed in Germany had vanished. It was back to the aggression, the fault finding and the droning voice. He knew better than anyone else. He gave Sarah an endless stream of advice and subjected her to a barrage of criticism on the new business. We were staying with her and her husband in their rented apartment in Yeronga and the personality clash between my daughter and my husband was becoming more evident by the day. He monopolised her laptop computer with his endless games of solitaire. His verbosity and abrupt instructions caused mounting tension. Sarah spent most of her time in her bedroom and I spent my time walking along the Brisbane River.

Sarah was searching for a house to rent. Her container was arriving from South Africa any day and she needed to get settled as quickly as possible. The new business needed urgent attention. Trevor's loud booming voice, issuing advice on every aspect, whether it was on the brand of toothpaste to buy or the area to live in, did nothing to alleviate the pressure.

On our second last morning, my daughter and her husband took me to breakfast at a coffee bar in Indooroopilly. Sarah took the wind right out of my sails. "Mom why do you stay with this man? Can't you see what he is doing to you? He undermines your confidence and treats you like a dog. Why don't you leave him?"

I had no answer. My life was in turmoil again. Was I doing the right thing to emigrate to a strange country with a husband that I did not love. I had headaches from morning to night. I asked her not to get involved – I would work it out.

Trevor and I caught the early morning flight to Sydney where we would change planes for our flight to Perth and then onwards to Johannesburg. My daughter's words were like a refrain, coming and going through my thought patterns.

We had just left Perth when Trevor made his abrupt announcement. "I am going on a safari to Zimbabwe when we get back. I have invited Karl to go with me. This will probably be the last time I see Zim so you can make all the other arrangements while I'm away."

I was shocked that he had not discussed this with me earlier. It was obvious that he had planned this trip well in advance and his friend Karl must have known all along. At first I felt angry and excluded. Why didn't he ask me to go along? Then I saw the benefit of having him out of the way. I could call in the furniture removers, get our belongings crated and containerised and I could start the process of selling assets. With him out of the way I could work in peace and tranquillity.

I decided that I would return to Australia within the next two months and needed to do a lot of work before then.

We were home for one week when Trevor and Karl left on their Safari.

CHAPTER EIGHT

Trevor's love life

It was while he was away that the phone calls started. She phoned one evening at 6.30 p.m. "Is that Verryn Grant?" "Do you know that your husband is having a passionate love affair?"

"My husband is 66 years old," I laughed. He is not going to have an affair, goodbye." I slammed down the receiver.

She phoned every day, telling me gory details about the affair. Where they were meeting and what they were doing. I felt sick. Trevor liked the company of women; he liked to tell them the stories of his vast wealth and basked in their admiration. But have an affair? I didn't think so. We had not had a physical relationship for the last six years of our marriage and there were many reasons for this.

Soon after we married I found out about his previous wife's wild and wanton love life. She was 30 years younger than Trevor, had come from a gutter existence and had led him a merry dance. She had openly admitted to all and sundry that she was oversexed and that Trevor could not satisfy her wild sex drive. She had conducted numerous affairs with a wide variety of men. She was also rumoured to have been involved in a lesbian affair. I started hearing the rumours of wild nudist parties and some of the men employed in our business were supposed to have enjoyed her favours.

I immediately asked Trevor to go for an AIDs test and he was furious with me. He went for the test, which proved negative, and I also went for a whole battery of tests to allay my fears of having contracted some or other disease from him. All my tests came back negative but I would not carry on with any physical relationship unless he wore protection.

This impacted on our married life and he became more and more distant. Looking back I now realise that much of his aggression towards me must have been linked to my rejection of him and I have to take part of the blame. However, when I heard about Trevor's sexual exploits I was so relieved that I had stopped the physical sharing when I did.

He never made demands on me – leaving me to sleep on my side of the king-size bed and tucking his sheet around him. I slipped into a barren marriage, only realising much later how lonely it could be.

I said he never made demands on me, except for one vividly-recalled episode.

We were holidaying on the Algarve with friends and had hired a beautiful villa in the hills of Lagos. As usual, when I chose the sleeping arrangements, I would opt for a room with two single beds. This time we had a room leading directly onto the pool deck, which jutted out from the edge of the mountain. The view was breathtaking and I used to leave the wooden shutters open at night so that I could lie and look at the twinkling lights of the city way below us.

It was about 5 a.m. one morning and I was sound asleep when I was jolted awake by a heavy weight on my chest. I could hardly breathe. For a wild moment I thought someone had entered through the open shutters and I was about to scream when I realised it was my husband. "What are you doing?" Squirming and shoving in panic, I pushed him away as hard as I could.

"I want to screw you..."

I could not believe what I was hearing and in a flash of anger screamed "Well I *don't* want to screw you, you revolting man!"

I got up, ran to the bathroom and knelt in front of the toilet. My head was spinning and I was nauseous.

I stayed in the bathroom as long as I could, had a hot bath and washed my hair. When I came out he was in the shallow end of the pool. Trevor was a weak swimmer and never went into the deep end. "Morning, love, come and join me."

The disgust must have shown on my face. I walked to the deep end and dived in, staying well clear of him.

The stupid bastard can't even swim, let alone screw anyone.

I felt as if I was dirty that entire day and could not get over his choice of words. That was the last time he ever made an advance to me.

Now, he was supposedly having a torrid affair with this rough-sounding woman who phoned daily. I think I felt a kind of comic relief.

CHAPTER NINE

Soweto

During the time when he was on safari, one Friday evening, I phoned Michael and asked him whether he was going to the club.

"I wasn't going tonight, but if you are going to be there, then I'll keep you company."

This private club was for exclusive members only and was housed in a luxurious mansion in our village. It had a small but select restaurant, a gaming room where the hardened gamblers spent hours on end, a small theatre where movies were shown and a regular cabaret act was performed. The members were mostly locals and we all knew one another fairly well. It turned out to be a very exciting night.

After having a delicious meal of the very best calamari and a bottle of Chardonnay, Michael and I were chatting to another couple when one of the more colourful characters, a Greek businessman, approached us and asked whether we wanted to join a group for the adventure of a lifetime. With hooded eyes Michael inquired as to the nature of the adventure.

It entailed travelling in a bullet-proof Volkswagen bus with an armed escort vehicle up front and another one in the rear. We would travel into Soweto for a night out in true African style.

"Michael, this sounds like fun, please let's go."

Now, for anyone living in South Africa in these times, merely driving past Soweto was hazardous, let alone driving into the sprawling black suburb which covered thousands of acres and is rumoured to be home to about three and a half million people.

There were daily incidents of hijackings, snipers shooting at passing vehicles, killings, mugging, rapes, you name it. Soweto is a dangerous place even for its inhabitants.

Here we were, a group of white party animals, deciding to take boredom to the hilt and test our indestructibility. Twenty of us decided to go and another bullet-proof vehicle had to be ordered. We left in convoy, about 11.30 p.m. The heavy-set bodyguard, complete with bullet-proof vest and machine gun, rode up front with the driver and proceeded to give us a strict lecture on what to do if we experienced 'a spot of trouble', like falling on the floor, covering our heads, remaining calm, not trying to see what was going on and obeying instructions to the letter, etc."

We drove in high excitement and as we got closer to Soweto, the tension was palpable. The turnoff from the highway was congested with traffic going in the same direction. Even at that time of night Soweto does not wind down – the pace hots up. I sat holding my breath and trying to act brave. The fact that our windows were tinted black did not give much comfort that outsiders would not be able to see that we were a bunch of Whiteys entering forbidden territory and risking our lives.

As we drove through the streets of Soweto, the shock and horror of the poverty was evident; even in the pitch darkness of some streets which had no lighting. The spirit of adventure was fast being dampened by the sight of little street urchins huddled in alleys and mangey dogs scrounging for food in the gutters. Skulking young gangsters plied their drug trade with some of them quite openly flagging down vehicles to push their trade.

We drove for 20 minutes in absolute silence and then started noticing the change in the environment. Here, the houses were huge with high walls and there was no evidence of squatter shacks.

We pulled up at a large walled enclosure – the walls could not have been less than three metres high and there were four armed guards standing at sold metal gates. Our driver flashed his ID and the remote gate opened. We were in and safe for the present! Were we? No one knew what to expect.

We drove up a large circular driveway and I noticed many BMW's, Mercedes and Audis, a Porsche or two and an assortment of Jettas and other saloon cars. No utes or battered vehicles here. This was most certainly the latest 'in' place.

Doormen dressed in bright red and gold assisted us from our vehicles and led us into the foyer of Ruby Red's Nightclub. The entrance was breathtaking in its splendour, most definitely 'over the top' but nevertheless like something straight out of Los Angeles.

As we entered, a beautiful young black woman holding a gold tray with cocktails, glided up to us and smiled her welcome. Her hair was braided and her make-up flawless. She had perfect teeth and exuded class. I could see the men in our group staring with open fascination at the beauty and grace of this woman and secretly wondered how many of them still harboured their racial prejudices of never touching a black woman.

We were led into the nightclub by a young man wearing a tuxedo and seated at a few tables nearest the stage. On stage was a black jazz band whom I later learned had become world famous. The music was wonderful and the talent on stage by far the best I had ever seen.

I sat back, lost in this strange world and drifted away on the sounds and the vibe of this forbidden place.

Michael, equally in tune with the music, seemed a million miles away. He never let go of my hand, drinking and smoking with his left hand only.

The jazz band came to the end of their session and a woman dressed in gold lamé took the stage. Launching into the latest love songs, she sang to piped music but her voice rose with such power that the lack of live backing was not even noticeable.

As she sang, more and more people drifted onto the dance floor. As if in a trance Michael guided me onto the floor and pulled me close. Oblivious to the interested glances from other members of our party, I gave myself up to the moment and drifted to the music. We danced and danced, not leaving, merely pausing for the singer to commence her next song. At the end of each song he bent his head and kissed me. The rest of our party was becoming more and more interested in what we were doing. I told him and he said he didn't care and pulled me closer.

I lost myself in time and place and held him close. Time had stopped and when the session ended we found ourselves out on the verandah staring at the man-made tropical garden lit with hundreds of strategically placed spotlights.

With his arm around me Michael led me to a sheltered spot and took me in his arms. He held me and I could feel his heart racing, keeping time with my own. My body felt liquid and numb all at the same time. He whispered my name, kissed my fingers one by one, stroked my arm and kissed my neck. I wanted to go home and make love to him. He had haunted my dreams for too long now and I knew without any reason for doubt that I loved him with a passion that I had never, ever experienced before.

I told him what I was thinking and it felt like the most natural thing in the world to do. He stood there gazing into my eyes and then he did what I would never have expected a man like him to do. He cried. Big round tears plopped from those deepest of dark brown eyes and made his thick black lashes look like clumps of moss found on the base of trees.

As he bent his head, I held his head in my hands, kissing his eyes and nose and whispering to him that we had nothing to lose – my life with Trevor was over. We stood for a while, staring at nothing, just holding hands and hugging now and then.

He led me back inside, seated me at the table and excused himself. I ordered more champagne wrapping myself in the rhythm of the band playing on.

Michael came back, sat down, lit a cigarette and did not say another word. Here I was, highly tense and needing of him and he was cool and remote. I could not understand the quick change in mood and spent a miserable hour waiting for the rest of the party to decide that we could now return to the safety of our homes. Most of the party had gone to the adjoining building which was a gambling club called Lucy Diamonds in the Sky. I knew from local experience that the gamblers felt nothing to continue their vice until the early hours of the morning. Eventually, Michael decided he had had enough. He had continued to drink and was, by now, quite drunk. He ordered the driver of our vehicle to depart with just the two of us and agreed to pay the premium price for this service. We needed the two armed escort vehicles and the charge was astronomical.

We drove in silence. Strangely enough, I felt no fear or threat of hijacking and fell asleep before we left the outskirts of Soweto. Michael woke me up when the bus pulled up outside of his home. I asked the driver to take me back to the club as my car was parked there. Michael said he would take me home and deliver my car the next day. His car was also at the club but he had another vehicle at home.

We walked into his house in stony silence and he made for the kitchen where he switched on the espresso machine. I sat in the black and grey marble kitchen and watched this cold and aloof man make coffee and smoke his cigarette. He was sobering up pretty fast and his mood was lifting. He now wanted to talk.

I wanted to go home – I was confused about his mood swings and did not feel like being courteous to him. I drank my coffee and asked him to take me home. "You can stay here tonight, I'll take you home in the morning."

"No I'm not, I'll phone the security company to escort me home." Taking out my cell phone, I turned my back on him.

I did not hear him come up behind me. The next moment the phone was out of my hand and flying across the kitchen where it hit the marble tiles. I stood there, speechless and afraid. I had never been subjected to violence in my entire life and this incident left me hollow with dread. He picked up the phone, checked it for damage and handed it back to me. "Come on, I'll take you to fetch your car and escort you home."

At the club, I jumped out of the 4 x 4 as quickly as I could and locked myself in my car. He pulled out behind me, following closely as I drove through the deserted streets to my home. I parked my vehicle, deactivated the extensive security system that governed our house and opened the front door. He had followed me up the front steps and stood there, not saying a word. His huge brown eyes were trying desperately to tell a story but I had no ears for it. My mind had closed off on the incident and I craved the oblivion of sleep.

He said something very strange. "If it's okay with you, can I see you tomorrow some time, so that I can tell you about my demons."

"I'll call you tomorrow, please leave now."

Waking to the call of the African loerie birds, which used to nest in the tallest tree in my garden, I knew that I was going to phone Michael as soon as I could. I wanted to know what his demons were. I called and we arranged to meet for breakfast at a quaint little restaurant on the banks of a lake.

CHAPTER TEN

Michael's story

With two swans, mates for life, floating idly on the water before us we ordered a breakfast of scrambled eggs and toast. I sat back savouring the freshness of the air and waited with a light air of apprehension to hear Michael's story.

"Linda and I met when we were teenagers. We went to the same high school and then onto university. I was being programmed to take over Dad's business and was doing my engineering degree. She was studying to become a teacher.

"We went out for two years and when she was 20 we convinced both sets of parents that they could trust us enough to take a holiday with a group of varsity friends who had booked a house in Ballito.

"As you know, my parents were very strict and moralistic and their so-called religious convictions made them apprehensive of us going anywhere without a chaperone. Her parents felt the same and we really battled to get our parents to agree.

"Well, I don't have to tell you what happened, Linda fell pregnant and we were terrified of telling our parents. We discussed all the options, eloping... no good, you still had to have parental consent under the age of 21. Running away... no good. We could not support ourselves let alone a baby. Abortion? Never, we agreed completely.

"At last, I approached my father. He went straight to my mother and she freaked. She ruled the family with an iron rod and boy did she blow her top. She ranted and raved, screamed and carried on about the disgrace, the stupidity, broken faith, you name it.

"It was then that I lost total respect for my father and started hating my mother. She insisted that Linda have an abortion and duly arranged the whole thing. Being an only child meant that I had no one close to go to for support and guidance. Dad washed his hands of the whole affair and became withdrawn, spending all his free time in his study.

"I will not discuss the actual abortion but it was done by a back street operator in Cyrildene and she botched it. Linda nearly died from the complications that set in and had to have blood transfusions. She was left with many gynaecological problems.

"We got married two years later when I graduated and I went straight into the family business. Linda had dropped out of university and was working as a clerical assistant.

"At this stage we did not know that she would never be able to conceive. After five years of being happily married, travelling overseas and building our dream home, we now wanted our own baby.

"Guess who was pushing the most – my mother – she wanted a grandchild and preferably a boy, an heir to the business.

"We started the round of doctors, specialists, homeopaths, you name it. This went on for many years and was tiring and stressful for both of us.

"After 10 years of marriage we were still childless and our relationship was deteriorating fast. Linda had started drinking socially with her girlfriends. She had not worked for a long, long time and was bored.

"I, on the other hand, had become totally involved in the business. My father took a back seat and I assumed more responsibility. I threw myself into the role of leader and challenged them on every issue, taking much pleasure in proving to both of them that I was better at the business than they had ever been.

"It got to the stage where I hardly spoke to my mother except for business discussions.

"Both Linda and I blamed my mother for our childlessness. I carried enormous guilt because I had allowed my mother to dominate me at the time.

"We decided to adopt and processed our application. The waiting period was 18 months. I became even more immersed in the business, leaving Linda to get on with life as a pampered housewife.

"I was so busy proving to my parents that I could supercede their expectations of me that I never noticed the deterioration in Linda's emotional state. The business had turned into an empire and my parents could not stop praising me for my efforts. This meant nothing to me, I hated both of them.

"When we were told that a baby was available for us to adopt, Linda and I took great pleasure in telling Mom and Dad that the baby was a girl. Mom hid her disappointment very well.

"She was three days old when we got her and she was beautiful. We named her Candice and both Linda and I could not get enough of her. We used to sit staring at her while she slept and the tears used to roll down our faces.

"Candice was five months old when the Nanny, Selina, phoned me to say there was a problem at home. I rushed home to find Linda blind drunk and suffering a breakdown. She was hospitalised and I had to employ a nursing sister to move into our home and supervise care for Candice.

"After six weeks of therapy Linda came home and bluntly told me that she no longer wanted this adopted child, that she wanted her own child or nothing and I better get rid of the baby.

"To say that I tried everything in the world to convince her otherwise is an understatement. I promised her everything I thought she may want; she would not budge. I knew then that the emotional damage suffered at the time of the abortion had now manifested itself and there was no going back.

"I had to have Candice removed and assisted in her re-adoption. Fortunately, she went to a loving home and I am in constant contact with her parents. I support her financially and always will.

"Linda went from bad to worse; she became an alcoholic, spent many months and years in time in and out of institutions. You know the rest.

"My demons are all too evident. I dislike the parent-child role. I feel threatened by anyone who has a close relationship with their children. I hated my parents until the day they died and now I know that I never really loved Linda. I don't even like myself."

I sat back, staring at the lake and the swans and tried to fathom out my reaction to this sad story. Could I ever really understand the tremendous trauma suffered and over such a long time?

Now I was starting to understand the coldness of this man. The fact that he could hold me and kiss me one minute and the next treat me as if I did not exist.

Now I understood all those cutting remarks about my very own daughters. He had so often told me that I was an over-protective, domineering mother and that my daughters were spoilt socialites. I understood, but only partly.

Our food had grown cold, neither one of us had any appetite left. We were unsure of what the next move would be. It was if we were in a boxing ring sparring with emotions.

My heart filled with a tenderness that spilled over into my very soul. I stared deeply and openly into his eyes and communicated my fears for his emotional wellbeing – he understood what I was trying to convey and voiced my thoughts.

I felt more reassured and knew instinctively that there was very little that I could think that this man would not be able to feel as he seemed to read my mind and know what I was doing. This telepathy had often cropped up in our business interactions and I suddenly realised that we were far too close as humans, too identical in psyche to ever be good for one another. I was born on the 11th November and he was born on the 13th November of the same year.

We were an old soul that had been split in two and reborn in two different forms.

I had this terrible feeling that if we ever became one we would destruct and totally destroy each other. For some unknown reason, a knowledge, older than time itself, warned me insistently that Michael and I would be dangerous for each other. He had his demons, I had my fair share. We were both obsessive in many facets of our lives but especially in the emotional arena. I had always been very jealous and possessive of my partner. Yes, even Trevor in the beginning of the marriage. This personality trait had caused me a lot of unhappiness and tears in the past.

I already knew that Michael was obsessively jealous and possessive. Could I live with this when I knew how destructive this emotion had been in my past relationships?

I was also a little afraid of Michael's temper and his controlled anger. At times, it seemed sinister. I would rather have someone rant and rave and get on with life than someone who kept such icy control – one never knows when it will snap. His coldness towards children made me wary. I adored my daughters. I could not imagine a life where I was distant from my girls and knew that Michael would create a life of seclusion, away from everyone.

Also, I knew deep down with Michael that it would be an 'all or nothing' situation. I would have to marry him and this I did not want. I had already decided that after my divorce from Trevor I would never marry again. More and more this fear of union with Michael sent me spinning into uncertainty. I questioned the reality of this love for him. It had developed over the past few years, had spun out of control the night before, but could it last forever?

We sat there for ages, staring at the water and when the heaviness of silence became too tangible I said we should go our separate ways as I had shopping to do.

"Verryn, think about what I have told you but don't question my love for you, please."

We hugged goodbye at our cars and I drove away with mist in my eyes.

That night I wrote him a letter.

Michael,
From when you bared your soul, I have been afraid.
Afraid of meeting my inner self and seeing my mirror image.
The feeling of staring at my soul is too scary yet strangely familiar.
How could we hide our secret fears from each other,
When we instinctively know what the other is doing and thinking?
If we both believe in fairies and Angels who is going to keep us grounded?
If I know what I am capable of doing to you, what comfort is there in knowing
That you are capable of doing exactly the same to me?
How can we both fly with the eagles and swim with the dolphins.

We would both drown in the blue depths and fly beyond our dreams.
Michael, you scare me with your intensity.
I know you are deserving of the very best.
My own history is too sensitive to project into the future.
I am afraid for us.
We are both too destructive – we both need gentle, carefree souls
Who will accept us,
Love us unconditionally and keep in touch with reality.
Dream on my very special Man
When I become elusive, it will be for both our sakes.
Perhaps Perth and Brisbane bring new light and a different dimension to our futures.
We can only wait and see.
Until then, please don't be angry.
I wish only for you what I wish for me.

CHAPTER ELEVEN

The threat

Trevor and his friend Karl returned from Zimbabwe on a Saturday evening. They were full of ebullience and adventure stories. I had played golf that afternoon and was not in the mood to listen to two men in their late sixties acting like grade school boys showing off about their madcap experiences.

I asked myself a little riddle. What's worse than a 66-year-old man acting like a 10 year old? Two sixty-six year olds acting like six year olds!

When Karl started talking about the beautiful blonde manageress of a game lodge in the bush and how smitten she had been with Trevor, I developed selective hearing and switched off. No doubt it was the mention of the latest Porsche and all the other luxuries that had helped capture her attention.

I made my excuses and went upstairs to bed. When Trevor eventually came to bed at about 10.30 p.m. he was extremely talkative. This was not unusual for him, he always hogged every conversation but usually he left me alone if I had gone to bed before he retired.

This night he seemed to want to get a reaction from me. I kept pretending that I was sleepy and not really able to concentrate on what he was saying. In the end I turned my back on him and pretended to fall asleep.

The next morning Karl left for his home in the Cape Province and Trevor busied himself with paper work and the odd game of solitaire. I decided to tackle him about the phone calls.

"Trevor, I've had a woman phoning me constantly whilst you've been away. She says that you are having an affair. Are you?"

"What are you talking about – are you being your usual neurotic self again?"

"Why would this woman be so insistent, she has given me details, I could check them out."

"Well, do that, you are stupid enough to fall for any con artist trick."

I left the house and drove to my daughter Kelly's apartment, which was only two kilometres away. I phoned a friend who had contacts. She had used a private detective to catch her husband out when she suspected he was having an affair.

Darren, the private investigator I spoke to, took details and asked me to deposit R5000 ($1250) in his bank account. I drove to the bank and transferred the money. Now I had to wait for the reports to come in.

It took three days before Darren had a fairly comprehensive report. Her name, address, marital status, occupation, where they met, what they did. I was flabbergasted. He faxed me a further account for R3000 ($750) and once again I transferred the money.

I walked into the study where Trevor was playing solitaire on his computer and stood in front of his desk. He ignored me as usual. I stood staring at this man whom I had tried to love and respect and all I saw was a fat, round little man who sat with bleary eyes and down-turned mouth, pushing buttons on a keyboard. He was intent on beating himself at the extraordinary game of solitaire! I wanted to laugh and had to force myself to think of him having an affair. It seemed so ridiculous. What woman in her right frame of mind would listen to all the bragging, the superior knowledge and the nonsense that this man imparted?

Yet, I had married him. I had thought I was in love with him. How could I blame this anonymous woman for feeling the same way? Undoubtedly, he was wining and dining her and showering her with gifts. She probably thought she had met her Prince Charming. What a shock she had waiting for her!

"Trevor, I have the proof. You *are* having an affair. I want a divorce."

"Then pack your bags and fuck off." He did not even look up from the computer.

"No, YOU pack your bags, this is my house, remember?"

"No, Verryn, this is my house and I will leave it over *your* dead body."

The veiled threat sank in, I felt the chill sweep over my entire body but was not going to show that I was intimidated. "What do you mean, are you threatening me?"

He lifted his head, looked beyond me, gazing at the tops of the trees viewed from the panoramic windows and smiled, it was more of a grimace, "Don't push me Verryn, just forget about all this crap and let's get on with our lives."

"No, Trevor, I want a divorce. I want us to go to the lawyers and settle amicably. I do not want to go to Australia with you. I want to start a new life without you."

He got up slowly, stretched his arms and rubbed his neck. Looking at his nails, he said, "Either accept me for what I am or leave. Yes, I may very well be having an affair but that's got nothing to do with you. She could be very young and you know how I feel about old women..."

My rage was uncontrollable and I screamed at him, "You arrogant bastard, who do you think you are? How long do you think you can keep a young woman, let alone an old woman happy? You are disgusting and they only want your money, can't you see?"

At the mention of his money, pride got the better of him. He was vain and arrogant and truly believed that all women found him irresistible. Suddenly, the ridiculous aspect of this situation made me laugh. Why was I even mentioning the so-called affair? I did not care if he was having an affair. I was secretly in love with Michael. All I wanted was to get out of this farcical marriage and start living again.

"Trevor, whether you are having an affair or not, I want a divorce. If you don't leave this house, I am leaving." I turned and walked out.

As I walked down the stairs to the lower level of the house, Trevor stood at the top of the stairs and his words reverberated throughout the mansion we called home. "If you leave this house, you are dead – I will have you hijacked or shot. Don't underestimate me you bitch!"

I stood at the bottom of the staircase and looked up into the face of Hell. His next words made me shiver as if someone had poured ice-cold water all over my body. "I will pay a mere R3000 ($750) to have you hijacked or better still, for a hundred grand I can arrange a drive-by shooting."

I walked back up the stairs until I stood looking into his face and I tasted bile in my mouth.

With extreme will power I forced myself to speak in a level tone and not to show my mounting fear. "Don't threaten me, I am going to the Police."

His dry, rasping laugh was ominous and the cruelty in his face struck with such force I had to close my eyes. "The gang I use have no fear of the cops, they rule and these Kaffir cops are useless anyway. Run down to the police station, they know me well. I have paid mega money to cops in my time, they wont even listen to you. They know who pulls strings. My money can buy doctors, judges, lawyers, you name it – a stupid cop in a charge office is a pushover."

I grabbed my bag from the kitchen counter and ran down

another flight of stairs to the front door with his laugh echoing in my ears.

As I sped down the road, not knowing where I was going or what I was going to do I felt as if his evil tentacles were eaching out to me and I was not wrong. At that very moment he was probably on the phone to his contacts and the reign of harassment and intimidation was being planned.

CHAPTER TWELVE

The bodyguard

Two years previously I had taken delivery of my new BMW and after only one month of driving it I was subjected to a frightening attempted hijacking. I had been reversing out of our garages when suddenly three men surrounded my car and I had a gun pointed at my head. At that very moment our neighbour, Nick, pulled out of his driveway and saw what was happening.

He drew his gun and shot wildly. The three hijackers ran for cover and I pressed the emergency telephone connection programmed into my car phone and alerted the armed response unit of the security company employed to guard our home. At the same time I pressed the panic button kept on my key ring and this activated the house alarm.

With all the noise and pandemonium the hijackers made off in their getaway vehicle and when the security company personnel arrived with sirens blaring and guns drawn, the robbers were well on their way to the next unsuspecting victim.

When we reported the incident the local police informed us that there was a Mozambican gang operating in the area and that the onus was on us to protect our assets and our lives. They did not have the manpower to be of any real assistance.

At that time Trevor was due to go overseas on a business trip and he insisted on employing the services of a firm of professional bodyguards to protect me whilst he was away. This company advertised their services as being select, discreet and of the highest professional calibre.

The man enlisted was young, about 28, average height and well built. He had steely blue eyes and close-cropped brown hair. He wore khaki waistcoats and loose shirts to disguise the bullet-proof vest and the shoulder holster. His name was Kirk and he never showed any emotion. He spoke in curt, clipped tones and gave instructions on how I was to behave in any unusual situation and made it clear that he took instructions from my husband only and that he was there to protect me not to humour me. I remember feeling very restricted and embarrassed at having this man follow me wherever I went. When Trevor returned from his trip and terminated the service I was so relieved.

This was the changing face of South Africa and more and more people were being forced to employ bodyguards for numerous reasons.

Now, having been issued with a direct threat, I contacted the company and spoke to the owner. I explained my predicament but stressed that I wanted protection from my husband who was a former client of theirs. He reassured me that their loyalty terminated at the end of each assignment and that I was now to be their client and my husband would not be able to influence them in any way despite whatever amount of money he offered. They were ethical and in their profession, ethics kept them in business, not the fast buck from bullies.

I booked a bodyguard for that night and for the next two weeks. At R2000 ($500) per day I would get the very best personal protection and if I wanted extended protection – say 24 hours, the fee was R3500 ($875) for 24 hours.

That entire night the young guard sat on the landing between the main bedroom and the guestroom where I had moved. Trevor had not said one word to either the bodyguard or myself. He chose to ignore the situation and retired to bed at nine o'clock.

The next morning, with a new bodyguard having taken over the day shift, patrolling the house and ensuring that Trevor kept his distance, I packed my clothes and moved them down to Kelly's apartment. My two maids, Valerie and Dora, were distraught and apprehensive about their future and I was powerless to reassure them. I had to hand this matter to the attorneys to resolve. One thing I could not do and that was to remain in the house with Trevor. I knew without a doubt that my life was in danger and I needed to get away.

The gang

The anonymous calls started the day I moved out. At first it was heavy breathing only. Then the cold voice of a man who asked whether my bodyguard was there. Unsuspectingly, I passed the cell phone to Dave, the guard on duty, only to hear him curse softly and switch it off.

For the two weeks that I had the guards nothing much out of the ordinary happened. We were aware that we were being followed at various times of the day and night by a variety of saloon cars, mostly white in colour and with darkened windows. I felt a little unnerved but tried not to overreact.

I had been to see a solicitor and had instituted divorce action. I was also finalising plans for another trip to Australia. I had to go and help Sarah with the plans to expand the business into another factory and she was very distressed at the news of what was happening in South Africa. She kept warning me to be careful as she did not trust Trevor and did not think that his intimidation was based on scare tactics. She thought he meant business and felt that he seriously had intent to harm me. I disregarded her protestations and kept telling her that Trevor was a bully and had no guts. How wrong I was. A bully he most certainly was but he also had the money to employ the most ruthless of operators and they had no boundaries.

Once my solicitor contacted Trevor's legal representative and told him what my divorce claim would be, in excess of nine million Rand ($2,250,000), the fight was on and Trevor spared no money in paving the way to destruction and fear. He loved a fight and had always bragged that he never lost a court case. This was giving him the adrenalin kick he needed to get through a jaded life consisting of his romance with an uneducated, rough-looking woman from the other side of the tracks and his passion for playing solitaire on his sophisticated home computer. He had no real friends and since we had sold the business his hangers on had no more reason to socialise with him. They could no longer benefit from his so-called 'friendship' and left him out in the cold.

I had become his obsession in a frightening, deadly way. He was not enjoying the fact that yet another wife had walked out on him and his pride was dented.

The lawyers were now working furiously; both sides recognised that this was going to be a costly divorce and the knives were drawn. My lawyer had advised the other side, in writing, of the death threats and the fact that I was forced to employ bodyguards and that we were reporting this to the police.

This action merely solicited even more bravado on Trevor's part. He phoned me late one night and it sounded as if he had been drinking. He was ranting and raving and the message was clear – I should get out of the country, go to my children in Australia and waive any claim to our joint assets or else...

The first incident occurred in a busy shopping centre on a Saturday morning. I had arranged to meet my friend Kate for breakfast at an Italian restaurant with a garden pavilion setting. It was very popular and we booked a table for 10 a.m. Kate had just returned from England where she had divorced her husband and was now contemplating setting up home back in Johannesburg.

That morning a new bodyguard had reported for duty and I

was on the brink of cancelling the contract as I felt that I was overreacting and making the situation to be more dramatic than it really was. The quiet, unobtrusive, casually dressed man named Shayne accompanied me to the centre and got out of the car before I parked it in the underground parking lot. He moved away, keeping me in vision at all times and I walked to the stairs leading into the shopping mall.

Kirk, who was one of the partners of the protection agency had phoned me the night before to give me the run down on Shayne and had assured me that he was highly competent and one of the best on his team. Kirk informed me that he had checked out the vehicles, which had been following us for the past two weeks and knew that they were from a detective agency in Johannesburg. He warned me to be careful as this agency was known to operate with untrained staff that were trigger-happy and employed the contract services of a notorious gang and he mentioned their name.

At that moment my heart had stood still. I had often heard Trevor referring to this gang by name and he had told numerous people that he employed them to teach people lessons and get matters 'sorted out'. I had taken what he was saying with a pinch of salt, as he was always verbose and once I realised that he had no self-confidence whatsoever, I assumed that his bravado was all an act, just trying to impress people.

As I walked through the mall last night's conversation with Kirk was forgotten and I was looking forward to seeing my friend.

Kate was already seated at a table and jumped up to give me a big hug. "Verryn, you look so stressed, I am so worried about you, tell me what's going on."

I started telling her the story of my departure from the house and noticed as I was talking that Shayne had seated himself at a table towards the rear of the restaurant. He sat facing me but had taken out a notebook and was busily writing in it.

Our cappuccinos arrived and we were lost in our world of friendship, catching up on each other's trials and tribulations. The table next to us was unoccupied and a movement caught my eye. A young man, very dark complexioned and with pitch black hair, had sat down. As I sat listening to Kate I casually gazed across at the man and was startled to see that he was staring directly at me, maintaining eye contact. I then saw that he was perspiring badly, the sweat running down his forehead and onto the collar of his dark blue T-shirt. I looked away and then back again. He maintained eye contact and when the waiter approached him I heard him ask, in an accented voice, where the toilet was. The waiter pointed to the rear of the restaurant and he got up, leaving his backpack on the table. As he walked slowly down the aisle to the toilet I saw the pistol tucked into his belt and looked across at Shayne.

Shayne was now reading a newspaper but he had turned his body towards me and held the paper at an angle so that I could see his face. He lifted his left hand and touched his ear. This was the signal that I had been briefed to mean 'keep watching me for further instructions'. The guy in the blue T-shirt had disappeared into the restroom and I told Kate what was happening and that I had to keep eye contact with Shayne. Kate knew that the bodyguard was somewhere around but did not know which patron he was. She carried on telling me about her saga, which equaled mine in some respects, and I listened but kept my eyes on Shayne who was now speaking on his cell phone but maintaining steady contact with me.

Suddenly, I saw Shayne stand up and without any further signs to me, as if he had flown across the restaurant, he was at my side and the instructions were bloodcurdling "Get up and walk in front of me, don't look back and DON'T RUN. Walk! NOW! "I cannot remember saying anything to Kate, I did as I was told and heard Shayne talking on the mouthpiece protruding from his collar. His right shoulder was touching my left one and he had put his right hand in the crook of my back and was propelling me towards an emergency exit in between two shops. It was then that I saw the other dark-skinned man walking towards us and I knew instinctively what was going to happen. I stopped dead and Shayne stepped in front of me, now pushing me backwards and as in slow motion I saw the man bare his teeth in a deadly grin and walk past us without even so much as a backward glance. Shoppers milled around us and some people were beginning to stare. Shayne reverted back to the shoulder bracing position and walked me briskly down the centre of the walkway towards the nearest exit. At that moment three casually dressed men appeared as if out of nowhere and surrounded us.

They hurried us out to a waiting vehicle and once in the car I started to calm down and couldn't help feeling a bit foolish. Had this incident been blown right out of proportion? Surely it could not have been a really dangerous situation?

We were overreacting. It could be circumstantial; the two men might not even be connected.

The driver of the car and Shayne were having a discussion and not taking any notice of what I was trying to say. The two men in the back seat with me were talking on cell phones.

My cell phone rang, it was Kate. "Verryn, let me speak to your bodyguard, there has been a strange scene here." She went on to tell Shayne that the first guy had come back to his table, a second dark-skinned man had joined him with much agitation and they had proceeded to talk in a foreign language. When the backup for Shayne had arrived, Kate was not aware that he had been called. He stationed himself at the entrance to the restaurant and had already reported the actions of the two men to Shayne. When they became aware of him their agitation increased and their argument became louder. They got up, throwing coins on the table for the single coffee, which had not been touched and walked out of the restaurant abreast of one another. Kate, whose father had been a captain in the police, sat watching this whole episode and was instantly aware of the man who stepped in behind them and tailed their every move from the restaurant.

As she sat there finishing her coffee, two other dark men, one of them blatantly wearing a pistol on his belt, came down the escalator right outside of the restaurant and walked towards the other two. All four of them stopped and continued their debate, unaware of the young guy in denim jeans who was keenly observing their every move but in a very discreet manner. They were so busy arguing that they did not even take notice of him. He was able to follow them and report back to Kirk. Two of the men were on black Yamaha motorcycles parked outside of the underground parking area where my car was left and the other two got into a red Honda Ballade with tinted windows and drove off. Kirk's decoy followed them and reported on their base, which was in the seedy suburb of Troyeville.

On arrival at Kirk's office we discussed this incident in detail and Shayne filled in the terrifying aspects of the story that I had completely missed. The first young guy, who sweated profusely, despite the fact that it was winter and dressed in a T-Shirt, his anorak bulging out of the backpack, had followed me from the car park.

Shayne had called headquarters and alerted them asking for standby assistance if needed. At the restaurant the young guy had walked away and disappeared into the crowds. After 10 minutes he had walked into the restaurant and straight for my table. I had been too busy talking to Kate and had not noticed that he had done a full circle around our table, scrutinising me. He had then sat down at his table and had acted nervously. It was when he went to the toilet that Shayne had received the information that the back up team was in the open-air parking and about to enter the mall. It was the right time to make the move and get out just in case.

As I sat listening to this 'de-briefing' session I felt the absolute unreality of the situation becoming too much to contend with.

Trevor and I had been married for eight years, we had been separated for three weeks. He could not be serious about harming me. Frighten me, yes, that he would do, but hurt me, never! I didn't hate him, I merely wanted to get out of this sterile and terribly lonely marriage and have a life. I only wanted my share of the assets accumulated during the course of the marriage. Trevor was a multimillionaire, surely he would not stoop this low?

"Kirk, I've heard enough. I think we are making this incident more dramatic than it really was. It could have been a co-incidence. I want to terminate this contract, I've had enough!"

"Very well, Verryn, but you are being very foolish. Your husband is an irrational man and he is playing an ugly game of harrassment and intimidation. The problem is he is using amateurish operators and these guys are the most dangerous. They get carried away and don't know when to stop. This morning's episode was a planned action and it went wrong only because the hit man was young and inexperienced. The outcome could have been serious."

"My personal belief is that Trevor Grant has taken a contract on your life and you are in danger."

"Nonsense, you are saying this because you don't want to lose a client – this is costing me huge sums of money!"

As the words left my mouth I regretted them. Kirk did not need to procure business by scaring his clients. His services were in full demand and he did not have enough manpower to contend with all the contracts on hand. I also knew that he operated his business on the highest ethics and I had grown to like and respect him.

"Verryn, I know you are stressed and feeling embarrassed and the decision is yours. I am not trying to hold onto this contract for money. Your husband is a dangerous man. We have done some digging into his character and hey, it's not looking pretty.

"Consider your decision carefully. Shayne will be on duty to protect you for the rest of the day – no charge."

As we drove back to the Mall, I questioned Shayne. "How could they harm me in a crowded shopping centre? You cannot shoot someone in such a busy place and not be seen and or even apprehended. What about all the eye witnesses?"

"This gang don't only shoot people, Mrs. Grant. There are many ways to skin a cat. Only last week a well-known businessman was assassinated at Johannesburg Airport. His assassin rubbed a highly toxic powder on his person and he died less than 12 hours later."

"This is ridiculous, we are in South Africa, not Miami."

"Just remember, your husband can afford to pay big bucks to hurt you. He may be trying to frighten you but if I were you I would listen to Kirk. He knows many people and has contacts. He is also very worried about you."

Shayne parked his vehicle at the shopping centre and told me to wait until he had checked my car. His examination of my car took ages and once again I was starting to get irritated by all the cloak and dagger actions.

"You can get in and reverse now."

He got into the passenger seat next to me and I noticed that he undid the flap on his holster. His actions were far more pronounced than before. He constantly checked in the side mirror, looked to the rear and scrutinised passing cars.

I drove home, parked underground and we took the elevator to the second floor, Shayne in close proximity to my every move.

I told him that I would not be going out that night and dismissed him. I needed to be alone and I needed to contact Michael.

Michael was in Taiwan buying machinery for his business in Perth. He did not know that I had left Trevor.

I dialled his cell phone number. He carried his phone day and night and took calls at any time.

"Michael Brent speaking."

"Oh, God, Michael, I need to speak to you. All hell has broken loose around me!" I was sobbing.

He listened attentively as I spilled out the sequence of events. He interjected now and then just to clarify a point. The line was so clear, it sounded as if he was up the road and not on the other side of the world. I began to feel calmer and once again, felt that I was overreacting.

"The bastard is not going to let you get away with this. You *are* in danger. He has a long record of getting even with people who have crossed him and his vengeance knows no bounds. I don't want to scare you..." There was a long pause and I knew this was one of those characteristic thinking moments when Michael drifted off into his own world. "Listen Verryn, I'll speak to Kirk and assess the situation. Phone you back in a few minutes"

"Do you want his number?"

"No, I have it – I'll call you shortly." The line went dead.

I should have known that Michael would know Kirk. He often used to hire bodyguards for his Japanese business associates when they visited his plant.

Ten minutes later Michael phoned back. "It's all arranged.

You will have protection until I get back in a week's time. A guard is on his way now. Don't you dare dismiss him. They will protect you around the clock. Just put up with the inconvenience."

This time it was Dave, shocking red hair, moustache and a jolly sense of humour. No sign of a gun but a tog bag carefully placed on the carpet in the lounge. He made sure the heavy metal security door was locked and then personally locked the front door. Going from room to room to familiarise himself with the apartment, he peered out of every window and closed blinds and curtains.

He picked up the phone, dialled his own cell phone and carefully listened, first on the one instrument then the other. I had followed him into the study that I now shared with Kelly and was about to call her to let her know what to expect when she got home. I was concerned that she would be unsettled by the presence of the guard during the night – she had got used to my daytime contract with Kirk.

Dave was speaking on his cell phone and I heard him giving the person my address. What now, I thought, can this get any worse?

"Why don't you take a kip Ma'am and I'll just amuse myself until they arrive to debug our phone."

"What do you mean, debug our phone?" I felt hysteria setting in again.

He shrugged his shoulders, "A soon-to-be ex-husband would bug his wife's phone. Your's is more likely to do it – he has the bucks I gather. So... we need to cut off his information link somewhat."

He read my face. "Don't look so shocked, your phone is bugged for sure. But help is on the way. Why don't you go and lie down. You look very tired. I could make you some tea?"

The debugging exercise was worth it. The sophisticated

electronic device was found in the basement in the Telkom service box. There would have been a bogus Telkom van parked within a kilometre or so and they would have been monitoring and recording every phone call, 24 hours of the day.

Dave instructed me not to use the home phone under any circumstances, even though it was now debugged, Trevor could implement further action and better devices. I was to use my cell phone at all times and on Monday was to get a prepaid sim card which had no number trace back to me.

I fell on my bed, too exhausted to worry about anything else, craving the oblivion of sleep.

CHAPTER THIRTEEN

Danger or intimidation?

The weekend passed in a blur. Kelly had taken the presence of the guard in her stride and carried on with her life as normal. I felt so foolish and so terribly guilty at having to subject her to such sordidness. She, however, kept reassuring me that she was only too glad that I had got away from Trevor. I was struck by her mature attitude and her incredible strength of character. She was the baby of the family yet so independent and strong.

The following Monday was spent in consultation with my lawyer and the advocates he had called in to assist with the divorce. Kirk had been on protection duty and he was called in to the boardroom to give an account of Saturday's occurrence. They sent formal notification to Trevor's attorney that we were handing over the report to the South African Police.

Earlier in the afternoon my dearest girlfriend, Shana, had called. "Come and have an early supper with us, we need to give you some moral support. Bring your bodyguard with you. We can have drinks around the pool and John can do his chicken peri peri thing." I gratefully accepted. Kelly was going to a movie and I needed company other than whichever guard was going to be on duty that night.

Shayne arrived to take up his shift and we left Bedfordview at 6 p.m. taking the Sandton highway. I felt quite relaxed and joked, "The good thing about having a permanent bodyguard is that one does not suffer the fear of hijacking."

"Never take safety for granted. There are many risks in our

country and bodyguards are only human."

I had to laugh at this contradiction and wondered if Kirk knew that young Shayne needed training in the marketing department.

The highway traffic had thinned out and the BMW purred at 140 kilometres per hour. Rod Stewart crooned his way through the 18 speakers in the luxury vehicle and I was enjoying the orange hue of sunset spilling over the six-lane highway.

The red Jetta screamed up behind us. I didn't even see it coming. They had no lights on and all I could see in my rear-view mirror was the fuzzy outline of two men. Their windows were tinted dark, illegally so.

Shayne, however, had been aware of them for some time but had not wanted to alarm me. The instruction was curt, "Put your foot down NOW, floor it and don't change lanes. Don't look behind you and do as I say!"

I heard the cocking action on the .45 pistol and knew we were in trouble. The 740 easily responded and picked up speed leaving the Jetta behind. I concentrated on the speedometer and barely heard what Shayne was saying on his cell phone. My car phone rang, Shayne pressed the answer button and Kirk's voice boomed over the automatic cutout to Rod Stewart. With constant dialogue between the two I carried out every instruction to the letter. By now we were coming up to the London Road off ramp, a notorious hijack point and entry to Alexandria, one of Johannesburg's most crime-ridden and violent black townships.

The truck travelling in the middle lane ahead of us suddenly changed lanes entering the fast lane. I was speeding up behind him and had obeyed Shayne's orders to take the fast lane. The far left lane had two cars travelling below the speed limit. There was nowhere to go. I had to wait for this lumbering truck to pass the vehicle in the middle lane, praying that he would quickly move back to the middle lane.

I felt the movement as Shayne undid his seatbelt and turned his body to the rear. His outstretched arm holding the gun pointed at the Jetta now catching up fast. With quiet instructions not to panic I swung back into the middle lane and then into the slow left lane. The Jetta was next to me, not more than a metre from my door. They were swerving in towards my car then moving out again. Each time they swerved towards the car I turned into the emergency stopping lane. Kirk was barking instructions over the car phone speakers and Shayne was now in the backseat, right behind me.

"Take the off ramp when I tell you, not before! We will pretend... NOW, go!"

I swung the wheel sharply and accelerated, feeling the thudding of the demarcation humps as we flew over the no-go area back onto the off ramp and sped left onto the access road to Alexandria. The Jetta had no option but to continue on its reckless path up the highway. They were beyond the off ramp when I swung over and for the time being we were safe from them.

"When I tell you to stop, slide into the passenger seat and get onto the floor immediately."

There was no time for argument about whether it was safe to stop in this dangerous area. I did as I was told. Shayne jumped into the driver's seat and I lay on the floor, numb with fear and shock. As in a tunnel, I could hear Kirk speaking to Shayne and knew that reinforcements were on their way to meet us.

At the police station, Shayne and two other team members escorted me into the charge office. The superintendent in charge was called and we were led into a side office. The middle-aged Afrikaans man wrote down the statement and opened a manilla folder. "Ja, this is the new South Africa. Life is cheap and if you got the bucks you can have your enemies knocked off. Mind you, you don't need much money, you can get a hijacker off the street and pay him 500 Rand."

As I lay in bed, much later, the tranquilliser starting to take effect. I resolved to leave South Africa as soon as I could and only return for the divorce action. I would make my plans in the morning.

CHAPTER FOURTEEN

Michael returns

Michael got back on the Friday. He looked tired. His trip had been hectic and he had the added stress of worrying about me. I had booked my flight to Australia for the Sunday night.

On the Saturday, Michael and I flew to Nelspruit for the day. He had a meeting scheduled with a game farmer who wanted to sell two rhino cows and Michael wanted to close the deal before these animals were sold to some obscure dealer and transported to unknown territory. His passion for animals always led him into these kinds of conservation deals and despite his fatigue he insisted in piloting us himself. We flew in his twin-engine Cessna. He had named this plane Roscoe and it was his favourite.

I had been so relieved when he said that we could dispense with the protection service for the day and noticed that his .38 Beretta was tucked into his belt, the khaki waistcoat not really covering it.

We arrived at about 10.30 a.m. and his meeting with the farmer was over by lunchtime. We had a simple lunch in a rustic little restaurant and then sat in their garden enjoying our coffees.

As we sat there in the beautiful surroundings with the sound of birds chirping and the lush greenery only found in the Eastern Transvaal, I wondered aloud how I was going to settle down in Australia.

This country, my country, had so much ethos and beauty.

Michael was lost in his own world. He often had very quiet moods and I had come to appreciate them and not to be threatened by them. He smoked his one and only cigarette for the day as he was cutting down. He had jokingly asked for my permission and then made a dry comment about his submissive attitude towards my commands.

As I watched him, sitting way back on the garden chair, eyes half closed, those incredibly thick black eyelashes almost touching his cheeks, I felt such a rush of affection and caring for him. I got up and walked around to his chair, putting my arms around his shoulders from the back. I kissed the top of his head and held him tight. He sat there, with his head resting backwards against my stomach and we stayed like that for ages.

Suddenly, he remembered something and started scratching in his pocket. He pulled out a tiny little packet wound with course brown string and handed it to me. I unwrapped it slowly, knowing deep down that this was a present with a message and when I saw the little gold symbol dangling from the finest gold chain, my heart felt like it was too big for my chest. I knew that this was a frozen moment in time and that a similar moment had been lived thousands of years ago.

The gold charm depicting the ancient symbol was the same as the one I had bought at Victoria Falls. I had since discovered what the symbol stood for. It was the African fertility symbol – it paid tribute to children and their importance in the greater scheme of things.

I looked deep into those brown eyes and knew that he was not mocking me. He was showing me, without words, exactly how deep his understanding was of my love and commitment to my three daughters. He was showing me his utmost acceptance of their importance and the knowledge that they took first place in my life.

Words failed me, he held my gaze telling me with his eyes

the whole story of his life, love and pain. I took his hands, holding them in both mine, the golden symbol nestling in the cocoon of love created by our flesh.

As I write this now, I am overcome with emotion and I grieve deeply for what could have been but never was.

The sunset was spectacular landing at Lanseria Airport that evening. The golden lines shooting up over the distant koppies of Pretoria made a ragged halo around the vista. We had been very quiet on the flight back. Michael kept his eyes on the runway as we taxied up to the hangar.

"We will emigrate to Australia. You help the girls to get their business going and I will grow my business in Perth. When your responsibilities are over, come to Perth. We'll be like the eagles, fly together and experience the freedom and beauty of that magnificent country."

"Yes, let's lay our souls bare to the destiny mapped out for us. I can't wait. I love you Michael."

I wanted nothing more than to give my entire being to him. Be with him, stay by his side, hold him, protect him and just love him unconditionally.

Our dreams had come together.

CHAPTER FIFTEEN

Back to Australia

I boarded the Qantas jet with red, swollen eyes and stowed my hand luggage in the overhead compartment. I did not even want a book to read. I wanted to sleep for the next 10 hours. The last 24 had been very emotionally taxing.

Kelly had been distraught at the airport, unusually so. She normally handled my frequent trips abroad with excitement and was always happy that I would be seeing her two sisters. This time, however, we had been through some rather terrifying times.

In a way I was relieved that I was leaving her to carry on with her life in a normal sense without the sordidness of Trevor's hate campaign to contend with. The novelty of having the bodyguards around us at all times had quickly worn thin and the lack of privacy had caused her to become withdrawn.

Michael had refused to come to the airport, as he did not want to impact on my time with Kelly. We had dined the night before and the experience had been romantic and funny. We were in a secluded corner of his favourite Italian restaurant and he had ordered a bottle of Moet. The owner of the restaurant, Alfredo, knew us well and when he brought the champagne to the table he placed two pewter goblets in front of Michael. "Special goblets for a special occasion, no?"

The cork popped and Michael carefully poured the sparkling wine. He handed me the vessel with twinkling eyes.

"I will forgive you if you dip your fingers into the wine in Sicilian fashion, you should check that your glass does not contain any foreign matter. You never know where Trevor has been lurking!"

Confused and not quite with it. "I'm sure he could not bribe your buddy, Alfredo has never liked him."

Entering into the spirit of the mood, Michael dipped his fingers in his goblet making an issue of stirring up the liquid. I decided to do the same – even though it was way out of character for me.

I felt the cold metal object and froze. Slamming the goblet down I looked in amazement at Michael.

"What's going on. You're playing games. There *is* something in my glass!"

Michael laughed, showing perfect white teeth, the moustache curling in that fascinating way.

I knew then what he had done. The diamond bracelet was curled in the bottom of the goblet. I fished it out and wrapped it in my napkin. The sparkling stones threw their light in many faceted directions and I held it out to him. He wrapped it around my wrist and fastened the catch. I touched the gold links, praying that our lives would be encircled with as much bright light as was contained in this gift.

I sat staring out of the aircraft window, holding my right hand over the bracelet on my left wrist and felt as if I was touching Michael and saying goodbye. I knew he was on his way to the game farm. He would be driving with his windows open, aircon off, savouring the fresh air of the Lowveld and yes, he would be thinking of me.

As the powerful thrust of the engines severed my link with my birth soil I sank back into the luxurious seat and closed my eyes. I would return to South Africa in eight month's time to fight my divorce in the Supreme Court of Pretoria. In the meantime, I was safe from Trevor's campaign of harassment and Michael would be joining us in Brisbane for Christmas.

I daydreamed and slept for most of the flight. In Perth we disembarked and I made straight for the Qantas lounge and freshened up. The flight from Perth to Sydney always felt much longer than the first leg of the trip. I was not looking forward to the hour's wait at Sydney before my connection to Brisbane. I would land in Brisbane at 11.30 p.m. and would be exhausted. The tiresome journey was made bearable by the excitement of seeing my two daughters and their partners. I had so much to tell them and was looking forward to my role in the business.

CHAPTER SIXTEEN

Emigration

The heat and humidity of the Queensland summer was draining my strength. I was also feeling very disorientated and could not shake the feelings of homesickness. Living with Sarah was not ideal. Despite the fact that they had purposely rented a four bedroom home with enough space for us to have our own study and living areas, I still felt cramped. I threw myself into the business and took on the role of managing director. My life had changed so dramatically and I was battling to come to terms with it.

Before living in Australia I had never ironed a blouse or even a table napkin. I did not know how to use an automatic washing machine and the numerous dials and buttons on Sarah's state of the art Miehle had me confused.

Life consisted of work, work, work. Gone were the days of luxury and servants at your beck and call.

'Back home' was starting to sound like a common refrain. Wherever we went we bumped into South African expatriates and the conversation was the same. We missed our fancy homes, our luxury vehicles, our maids and gardeners, our businesses and all the money! In Oz we had to come to terms with the difference in business practice, the way to manage staff, the fact that you had to put in a full day at work and then go home to do the chores.

In the early days we seemed to come across far more negative emigrants than those who had settled and were happy in their new country. It was definitely a case of negative karma attracting further negatives.

We condemned the attitude of the Australian workforce. We could not understand why they did not want to work hours and hours of overtime so that they could earn lots of money. We could not believe that fishing and surfing could take preference to earning double time in your wage envelope.

Where we came from money was paramount and possessions gave you status and security.

As the weeks went by we learned more and more. We started to understand that our labour force enjoyed their home lives and were only prepared to work the mandatory hours per week. We learned to motivate without threat and gained respect and loyalty. The productivity in the business started picking up and turnover was escalating.

We started enjoying the freedom that this wonderful country offered; the beautiful landscapes and friendly people. We were settling down and suddenly we were meeting many other South Africans who were so happy in this new land of ours.

CHAPTER SEVENTEEN

Christmas in Oz

Michael and I kept in contact. He phoned me every day. He had been in Namibia negotiating a contract for the South African business, had been to Zambia for a week and he was then going to Taiwan to look at equipment for his new business in Perth. He intended coming to Brisbane to spend Christmas with my family and me.

In early December I flew to Sydney for business meetings and booked into a hotel overlooking Darling Harbour. I spent two days working and decided to remain there for a weekend break. I love Sydney and have some close friends who have lived there for many years.

Charles and Annette, my friends, had been dying to see the show at the Imax. It was called 'Africa – the Serengeti' and we decided to go to the late show on the Saturday afternoon.

It was an incredible documentary of the migration of the animals from the Masai Mara in Kenya to the Serengeti in Tanzania. I was overcome with emotion and longing as I sat, spellbound, throughout the show. I had spent a wonderful holiday in Tanzania a couple of years before. As we walked out of the theatre into the milling crowd I wondered how many people seeing that show would truly understand the magnitude and magnificence of that wildest of wild country.

We walked along the promenade and there was a bright and colourful carousel erected to the left of the theatre. On impulse we decided to lighten our mood and we laughingly climbed onto the carousel, joining many adults with their partners and children. That is the beauty of Australia, the people know how to have fun and do the most simple and childlike things. No one condemns you for enjoying yourself.

As I sat on the bright yellow horse with cracked paint and wildly painted eyes fringed with extra long plastic eyelashes, I had one of those shivers that run down your spine and you remember the old saying that 'someone has just walked over your grave'. A vision of Michael flashed into my mind and I suddenly knew that I should get back to the hotel and phone him.

I made my excuses of being very tired and said goodbye to my friends. Rushing into my hotel room I threw my bag on the bed and frantically dialled Michael's cell phone number. His voicemail came on. This was unusual for him; he kept his phone switched on at all times. I had a number for the hotel in Taiwan and punched in the number.

"Mr Michael Brent please."

"Ah, Mr Brent not available, sorry." She sounded vague.

"I am calling from Australia, please put me through."

"No can do that, Mr Brent not here. He ill to the hospital."

My head pounding, the hollow echo over the line making me more distracted. "Where is he – give me the number please. It is very important." I held on whilst she looked up the number of the private clinic he had been taken to. Frantically I dialled the number, not caring about the six-hour time difference.

The male voice answering must have recognised the panic in my voice and put me through to the private ward. Michael sounded groggy and very ill. He told me he had collapsed at a business meeting earlier in the day and that the specialist called in was arranging for tests to be carried out within the next few hours.

I was devastated and felt so helpless. Here I had been riding on a stupid carousel when he was lying in a hospital bed, so very ill! I cried and cried and phoned him again and again, telling him that I wanted to be with him and to help him. He kept reassuring me that he was in the very best of private hospitals and that the doctors all seemed to know what they were doing. The only problem they had was the difficulty in communicating.

I did not sleep a wink that night and when I phoned the next morning he told me that they were going to treat him for an unnamed tropical disease. I left Sydney in the afternoon and Sarah met me at Brisbane airport.

I spent two agonising weeks worrying about Michael. Each day when I spoke to him, no headway had been made. He was not getting any better and the doctors seemed to be getting confused. Eventually, Michael phoned an old friend of his, a physician who had emigrated to the United States, and asked him to fly to Taiwan and diagnose his illness. Theo made the trip and diagnosed Michael as suffering from malaria, which he believed, had been contracted when he was in Zambia.

Theo accompanied Michael back to South Africa and booked him into the best private clinic in Johannesburg. The most respected team of doctors were enlisted to run further tests.

Michael endured weeks of tests and I spoke to him daily from Australia. He never let on how desperately ill he was. He kept telling me to concentrate on the task at hand and that he would make it to Brisbane for Christmas. His flight was booked for the 23rd December.

On the 20th December Michael phoned me. "Verryn, I can't come to Australia. I'm sorry to let you down"

"What now, Michael?" My dissapointment made me hoarse.

"I am going to die, Verryn. I have eight months to live."

"That is a sick joke, don't be a jerk. What are you playing at?"

"I wish I was playing my love. This time it's no joke. The death wish was to fly to the end. This aviator has completed his hours barring 32 weeks if I'm lucky."

As I held my breath, clutching the phone, he told me the diagnosis. I could not cry. My mind was dead, my body numb.

Michael went to his game farm for the Christmas week. His loyal staff were told of his illness and they cared for him with all the love and dedication of children knowing that their father and protector was going to leave them forever.

I drifted through this festive season, not wanting to participate in any partying or socialising. I spent much of my time in my bedroom reading and making my plans to return to South Africa in early January.

At 12 midnight on the first of January – Australian time – I phoned Michael and told him it was 'our' New Year. His and mine. As new Australians we were to make our wishes for the coming year. He humoured me and I told him that I would phone him eight hours later at midnight South African time to wish him a happy New Year. When I phoned him at 8 a.m. Australian time, his answering machine was on. He had gone to sleep.

For the next two weeks I spoke to him several times a day. Some days he was feeling healthy and fit and working hard at selling his house. He was packing up his vast art collection and selling his Persian carpets. Other days he was back in the clinic and often too ill to talk to me.

I floated through a haze of love and pain, fear and hope, communication and rejection. Some days Michael would refuse to take my calls. He was very angry at the world in general and locked himself away in his study. I felt a desperate need to get back to South Africa and held onto the belief that somehow, if we were together and I could look after him, he would not die. I believed that my love could make him better and prolong his life. He kept telling me that we were bound together forever, that we were one soul and that we would fly with the eagles and swim with the dolphins. I gradually learned to accept this and held onto my love for him whatever the frame or image it must take.

I made my plans to return to South Africa and had booked a Saturday flight.

My phone rang at one minute past midnight on the Friday morning. Thinking it was Michael I grabbed the receiver. "Hello, darling".

The cynical laugh echoed down the international line. "Darling? How did you know I was calling? Have you changed your mind about me..."

The anger and disappointment reverberated in my voice "What do you want Trevor. I was not expecting you to call!"

"Well, then, you must have a lover calling you at midnight hey? Tell me about him. Anyone I know?"

"What exactly do you want, I am putting this phone down."

"I know you are returning to South Africa and I want to give you some clinical advice, Verryn. Listen carefully. I have framed you. If you come back you will be arrested at the airport and jailed. Best you allow me an uncontested divorce and you walk away from your money claims."

"You Bastard! Do you think you can get away with this? You cannot play God with people's lives. Leave me alone!

"Okay, catch your flight on Saturday and be warned. Rather, be afraid... but then again, it's your call Verryn. You never played a good game of poker did you?" The despicable laugh sent shivers through my body. I slammed the phone down, unplugged it at the wall and ran for the toilet. Physically ill and shaking, I sat in the darkened lounge and considered his threat.

He couldn't get away with this. Or could he? He had done awful things to people who had owed him money or who had dared to antagonise him. Could he really have the power to do this and with what ammunition. I had not done anything wrong. What was his game?

I decided not to discuss this call with anyone and would ignore his ridiculous threats. He wanted to keep me out of the country so that he could walk away with all the assets. I was not going to let him get away with it.

CHAPTER EIGHTEEN

Back on South African soil

As the Qantas jet landed at Johannesburg International I had that strange feeling of foreboding and deepest knowing. I walked into the waiting arms of my darling daughter Kelly and held her hand as we walked to the car park. It was 7.30 p.m. I had been travelling for more than 22 hours and I was dead tired. At the apartment, I went to bed immediately and slept like a log.

Early the next morning I went to the clinic where Michael had been for the past few days. Walking into the private ward, clutching a bunch of yellow roses and a Louise Hay book I couldn't wait to see Michael.

He was lying with his face turned to the wall. Those impossibly long eyelashes touching his cheeks. His unlined face was tanned by the African sun, thick black glossy hair tousled. His one hand, resting on top of the pale blue cover, looked as if it had been sculpted by an artist who craved perfection in hands and nails. Michael's hands had always fascinated me.

I stood there, watching him and could not utter a word. It seemed like forever and then he stirred, turned his face and opened those deepest of dark brown eyes, now cloudy with drugs or pain. As he focussed on me his face creased into that lopsided, quizzical grin that used to turn my stomach upside down. He held up the hand that I had been staring at. Putting my gifts down I took his hand, bent down and kissed his eyes, cheeks, nose, forehead and his mouth.

They had shaved off his moustache; he looked so young.

Words would not come, not from him, not from me. We stared and stared, we grinned, we smiled, we became serious. Our eyes were doing all the talking as usual – and we had so much to say.

I knew that if I started crying he would tell me to go. He would close off and shut me out. I started finding words, inane words like, "So you keep me in Oz whilst you have the best time out – lying here with all these attractive nurses pandering to your every whim. In absolute luxury, two phones and a cell phone! Just moved your office in here I see. Where are the paintings Doll? And, who, by the way, gave you permission to shave off the trademark? The moustache made you look intelligent."

He laughed softly, the sound gave me a warm feeling all over. "So where's the accent Doll? How come you haven't developed the Brisbane lilt? And what about that haircut, get on the phone to your designer hairdresser immediately!"

Backwards and forwards, the easy banter carrying on, we drifted into more serious conversation. Filling each other in on the latest developments in our lives. Me telling him about the two girls in Australia and the business; him telling me about Linda and her life in Portugal with Luis. We skirted the main issues, neither one of us wanted to talk about Trevor or the illness. Soon we were laughing about current affairs in South Africa and the happenings in our social circle.

I held onto his hand throughout this discussion. It felt thin and cold. I would squeeze it to give emphasis to something I was saying and he would return the pressure with his usual strength. I couldn't help my thoughts. This is all a mistake; he is such a healthy man. There is nothing wrong with him. He can't die. Doctors make the wrong diagnosis all the time.

The nurse came in and asked me to leave. I had been there

for three hours. I kissed him and told him to phone me at any time of the day or night. My cell phone would be on. He told me to do the same.

I walked to my car in near blindness, tears streaming down my face. I sat with head in my hands, unable to drive away. Staring at one of the blue curtained windows, hoping it was his.

I drove home and wrote him the first of many letters. I never gave them to him.

Michael, my eternal soul mate.
I am losing you – you are not deserting me.
Merely going forth on the journey
we ultimately take on our own.
I thank you for your wonderful being.
For all I have gained from knowing you –
and loving you.
I have learned so much about the lore
of our beloved land.
I have experienced feelings that I never dreamed of.
I have been able to express myself like never before.
I have truly loved.

Our friendship, our togetherness, our love
has been quite lonely, for want of a better word.
You were there for me, the sad times, the fun times.
Through the harassment, the intimidation, the fear.
You stood firm and gave me support and advice.
What madness prevailed, why were we being so strong.
What was the shroud clouding our vision.
Why did we not take the plunge and swim with dolphins.

Michael, from the moment I heard about your pain,
I convinced myself that I could make you better.
That we could walk into the sunset together.

I know now that this was not meant to be.
Now, looking back, I cannot understand
the wasted opportunity.
Why did we not release the hold on reservations
and go with the flow.
Deep down I must have known, (you knew too)
that you were going to leave us,
and the pain of loss would have been too much to bear.
It is no less, even now.
Right now it is too much to contemplate
but I become stronger
because of your awesome strength.
Tomorrow I am going to sit with you
and we are going to talk Africa talk.
I will ask Vusi to call on his ancestors to light your path.

Michael, whenever I look at that statue
called the 'Family'
Bought at Vic Falls, it now has pride of place
in my study in Oz,
I will relive in infinite detail our morning in Harare and
the flight to the Falls.
I will always remember the 'cloud rolling' and will
vividly see your face,
Radiant and confident as you flew high above our
Beloved Land.
I will never forget the ostriches on the plains and will
live the walk at Elephant Hills.
The pathway at Mashatu is also etched
into my mind forever.
Laced with emotion, the sunset wove into our blood
and the lion in the clearing
told us that this is our Land (his and ours)
and that he is our soulmate

Michael, I remember your face as we sat
in the Land Rover watching a line of caterpillars
crossing our path before we could carry on – what
intensity and affinity with nature of our bloodroots.
How can I leave this country?
How can I now leave the hovering souls
of my departed loved ones – and you too-
Will I ever feel the pulse of land in Australia?
Michael, I am now doubting myself and my future –
Please don't leave me.
I am struggling with your going.
Now my mind is arid and my heart doesn't beat.
Michael, come back to me often, walk next to me
and yes, if I stay in Oz
whisper the words of encouragement
and lace my heartstrings with new loyalty.
Michael, this little poem is for you –
In the language of our Land

In my hart en siel sien ek skaduwees
Van pyn en verlore drome
Ek voel en klou aan die stukkende drome
My hart is vol van die verlede
My siel gee vlug aan verdriet en verlies.

I wish I could turn back the clock
and why can't we be those
'Avid, ardent Aviators' again.
Right now I am feeling so angry with you and tomorrow
I will tell you my thoughts – hold your hand
and you will give me pearls of wisdom.
I am so tired and hurting so much.
Goodnight my darling.

CHAPTER NINETEEN

Coming to terms with death

The next day I got to the clinic at 9 a.m. I walked into the ward to find the bed empty. Rooted to the ground, my mind spinning, had he died? Where was he? Oh Dear God – not now, not yet, there is still too much to say.

A nurse walked up behind me. "Mr. Brent is in ICU, he had a bad night."

"Can I see him, please, I have to see him, now." The desperation in my voice even shocked me. She looked away, "Please come back in an hour, the doctors are with him now."

I sat in the waiting room, not seeing anyone else or caring. I felt as if I had stepped into a vacuum. I felt very cold. I had the little gold fertility symbol in my bag. I took it out and fastened the chain around my neck. I stared at my bag and all I remember seeing was the designer logo and I repeated the name to myself over and over as if it was a mantra. By doing this I could make the world go away. I took out my little notebook and started writing another letter to Michael.

Michael, I hold my heart in my Fendi.
I walk, feeling numb – I sit, feeling numb.
If I were to wish anything right now, it would be
us sitting in the lookout at Falcon's
and telling each other childhood stories.
What absolute affinity we have,
all those mixed emotions, those terrible fears,
the hurts, the embarrassments,

We have them all and we are identical.

Why did we not allow ourselves the freedom of choice?
Why did I sacrifice for Trevor's sake –
Where did it get me?
Perhaps both our lives would have been different.
You would not have become ill.
It is our own inherent Scorpio natures
that screw up our lives.
I am sitting here waiting and will not go
until I can tell you how much I love you
and that you are going to get well.
We are going to fly into the sunset together
and find our own eagle's nest.
Come back darling.

I waited for two hours. Eventually the same nurse came looking for me. "You can go into ICU now, Mrs. Grant. Please change into a sterile gown and stay for five minutes only."

I went in with total conviction that Michael would smile and talk to me. He was fast asleep. The drugs had not worn off yet and he did not respond to my whisperings. I sat there for five minutes holding his hand. I left when they called me out and drove home in a haze of pain.

It was almost midday, I got under the duvet and went to sleep.

I slept until early evening and then had a light dinner with Kelly. I watched television and phoned a few of my girlfriends. Everything I did was aimless, with no real intent, I couldn't focus on anything.

The next morning I woke to the sound of a Loerie bird. For some reason it gave me hope. I knew Michael would be feeling better. After a rushed breakfast with my daughter I headed for the clinic. As I walked through the double doors of the hospital I knew that Michael would be out of ICU and back in his private ward. What remarkable stamina this man had. He had immense willpower and strength of mind. He was propped up on four pillows reading the newspaper and heard my step as I came down the passage.

With a beaming smile he patted the bed indicating that I should sit. I bent down and kissed him full on the mouth and then gave him hundreds of little kisses all over his face and hair. He was laughing and shrugging me off when the nurse walked in. She smiled and made a hasty exit.

I sat where he wanted me to and from this position could maintain eye contact at an even level. We stared into each other's brown eyes. "Michael, did you know that you were going to die young?"

"I've always known, that's why I used to take such chances when I was flying – almost like a death wish."

"But why, why would someone with everything to live for have such negative energy inside of them?"

"Because I never wanted to become like my father – old and pedantic and with no joy in life."

"So, you're telling me that you created your illness and you have achieved your goal!"

"Not quite, I wanted a bit more time and yes, I wanted some happiness before I left this planet."

"Does that mean that maybe, just maybe, you considered me as part of your happiness?" I waited with quiet longing for him to acknowledge the importance of our love. He turned away and I walked around the bed so that he was forced to look at me. He was crying, those impossibly beautiful brown eyes clouded with sorrow. He looked like a little boy, lost and frightened. His anguish was tangible. I knelt down and held him. Rocking him, stroking his face and kissing his hair. I loved the smell of his hair, it reminded me of the flowering shrubs growing outside of his wooden deck at the game farm. I am sure that he used to distil those flowers and have his own shampoo made – I would not have put it passed him.

Michael then became serious and we went into a lengthy debate on what should happen with his business in Perth. Who should take over the management of his Wildlife Trust and who would look after Linda and Candice when he was gone. There would be trust funds for both of them. Despite the fact that Linda was married and living in Portugal, he still considered her to be his responsibility.

He asked me if I would be co-executor of his estate. The other executor would be Gavin, his accountant. "No, Michael, I cannot get involved in anything as time consuming as that. I have to help my girls with the business and need to settle down – put down my roots." I had enough problems with the pending divorce. Litigation in the Supreme Court was a lengthy procedure and I knew that for the coming months I would be heavily involved in legal matters.

"Your girls always come first! When are you going to wake up and realise that you come first. Your daughters are adults, they don't need Mommy holding their hands and guiding them!" Once again we were locked into a battle of words concerning my children. Michael just could not understand the parental bond.

Hours went by. The nurse brought his lunch and I shared it with him. I did not want to leave his side for a minute. Each precious moment counted too infinitely. We ate the chocolates one of his visitors had brought and we shared more life stories. When the sister in charge asked me to leave as they were taking him to theatre for tests I kissed him goodbye and said I'd be back later that evening.

When I got back to the clinic at 7 p.m. Michael had slipped

into unconsciousness and the curtains were drawn around his bed. Two nurses and a doctor were attending to him. He had developed an allergy to one of the drugs administered that afternoon. He was very ill.

This sudden change was too much for me. That afternoon he had been full of life and vigour and now he was unconscious!

What kind of hospital was this! I was so angry and needed to vent my feelings.

Gently the nurse took me aside and explained what the illness was all about. How the regression could accelerate and that the 'highs' experienced were also part of the course it took.

I left there in deep depression and sat in my car staring at the sky. There were far too many bright sparkling stars in the Universe. "You don't need another one up there, God. Let him live, PLEASE."

I went home and wrote him yet another letter.

Michael,
I am losing you.
Soar free and painless.
Your heart is held by many.
You will never be forgotten.
Never out of our vision.
Your strength and persona
will fill every space in my life,
and I will always hear your voice.
I will see through your eyes the art and other collections.
You taught me appreciation, you taught me sensitivity.
You brought me a brand of loneliness –
I could not always reach you.
I know your secrets, some of them.
Share them and will never tell them.
I am crying for what might have been

but don't know the truth.
Sometimes my heart feels like it is
bleeding with pain and loss,
and I make light of it – pretend that
you are not going away,
that you will stay, my loyal, faithful, strong Michael.
Looking back, I know that there was infinitely more.
The walk on the jetty, picking up identical stones –
was that the sign?
You said something to me on a flight one day,
then changed your mind and became cold
and distant – do you remember?
You held my hand as we walked
through tall grass once – I stopped you,
wrapped my arms around you and kissed you,
Do you remember?
I loved you deeply but you were like ice.
If you had allowed me to love you that day,
we could have faced this together as one.
Why was this so difficult – was it my fault
because in the beginning I said
I was afraid of the intensity?
Why did you not take the lead?
I cannot imagine a future without you.
It seems so unfair.
My Darling, I ask that you cross the oceans
with the Dolphin Prince,
and then fly with the Black Eagle,
high over Brisbane and look for me.
Bless my life and let me always remember.
Michael, if you are to die here and your ashes scattered
on Falcon's Rest,
how am I going to talk to you from Australia?

Perhaps I can't go and live there –
Perhaps I should stay here.

After writing this letter I sat on the balcony with a bottle of Sangria to keep me company. Strangely I felt that I was coming to terms with Michael's illness and I was still under the impression that he had about five months to live. I started making plans.

I would take him to Falcon's Rest. We would employ a private nursing sister. We could even go and holiday at Chaka's Rock on the Natal north coast. We both loved that stretch of coast and each had a holiday home there.

I sat there for hours and eventually went to bed at midnight. At 2 a.m. I woke with a start – I had been dreaming and I needed to write.

Last night, with Sangria as my companion,
I watched the twinkling stars
on the Johannesburg skyline.
I saw the ghosts of my parents float free above the city
where they spent most of their lives.
I heard my Dad's voice – "Walk bravely
and do not fear the future."
I remembered him telling me
never to amble through life but to jog.
I felt like going for a jog but it was too dangerous.
Then I went to bed and had two dreams.
I dreamed I was running a marathon
with an unknown black man.
We ran through hotels and guest lodges
and eventually he stopped,
took off his shoes and told me to run on...
The second dream was at Chaka's Rock.

I walked to the water's edge and it felt warm.
As I went further the water got colder and colder.
I was in deeper water and wanted to get back to shore.
I could not see land and started sinking.
Then I felt myself being lifted clear of the water,
looking down on the waves,
now becoming awesome and wild.
I woke up.

I interpreted the dream as:

The black man signifies my roots and as I run with him, my stamina is greater than his. He tells me to go forth but he remains.

The water is the known being left behind for the unknown,

Leaving warm liquid melting comfort for colder, unknown territory.

Experiencing the fear of seeing your Land fade away and disappear.

Feeling of drowning and then surging free.

Floating and looking back on those waves, which are very threatening but also powerful.

Knowing that you are free and flying high.

My prayer to the Universe

Dolphin Prince you plummet the depths.
Your grace and beauty never fades.
You live the star-filled night.
Grow each day wiser and more true.
You send signs to mere mortals,
of hope, courage and infinite love.
As I wait to see you in a Land faraway,
I hold dear your image as you play

and speak off Chaka's Cliff.
Take my memories with you – I have made promises
to keep and all my whisperings
on broken sand castles I leave with you.
I see the hermit crabs and eels in Chaka's Pool
and my heart misses a beat
For the memory of rugged cliffs, orange flower trees
and tiny mossies (little sparrows).
I see the whale that got lost
and know that you did all in your power
to guide him back to the depths and freedom
of your tranquil world.
I know that each day you travel, playing the waves
from Phinda to Umhlanga to Durban and back.
Always passing the flat at Chaka's Rock.
My heart floats with you and my dreams spill over.
Take my history with you and allow me to call on you
for pieces of the past, fragments to hold
and to whisper my dreams and fears.
Take my love of Africa and keep it warm and glowing.
Hold my being in your soul, and as you roll
in these turquoise waters,
send me visions of where I was.

Perhaps I should explain this part. I owned a beautiful holiday flat right on the beach at Chaka's Rock. When we were on holiday there, every day, sometimes twice a day, we would watch the dolphins as they swam close to shore on their journey south towards Durban. They would gambol and play and would return later in the day. I always imagined that they lived in deep water, close to the Phinda Reserve so that they could silently communicate with the wild animals in the bush and tell each other about their experiences of the day.

Michael also owned a holiday flat in Chaka's Rock. It was about a kilometre away from mine. He hardly ever spent time there as he was passionate about the bush and spent all of his holidays on his game farm.

I used to try and spend every Christmas and New Year at the coast. The elder two girls, when they were still in South Africa, always stayed there with us. Kelly used to adore these holidays and loved being with her sisters.

The only dampening effect on these holidays used to be Trevor's moods. He used to sit for hours playing solitaire with a deck of cards and we were never allowed to open the sliding doors onto the balcony as the sea breezes used to disturb his cards.

We used to leave him sitting there and go for long walks on the beach or to swim in the tidal pool right below the flat. The marvellous creatures living in this pool kept us spellbound for hours – eels, hermit crabs and the brightest coloured little fish.

CHAPTER TWENTY

The arrest

It was Thursday morning. Kelly and her boyfriend had left home at 5 a.m. The long drive to Ballito on the northern side of the KwaZulu coast would take them five hours. They were spending the weekend with his parents at their holiday flat on the beach. I got up soon after they said goodbye to me and made myself a cup of coffee.

Contemplating the day ahead, I decided to take a hot bath and get to the clinic early. Michael had been very ill during the night. I had phoned him at midnight and his cell phone was switched off. When I got through to the night sister on duty she told me that he had taken a turn for the worse and that he would be sedated.

At five to six the intercom for the main door in the reception foyer rang. I did not think it was too strange as I assumed that Kelly had forgotten something and instead of driving into the basement parking had parked at street level. Wrapping a towel around my wet body I ran to the hallway and picked up the intercom phone.

A man's voice, strangely hollow, enquired whether I was Mrs Grant. "Yes, what is it?"

"Open the door Mrs Grant, this is the Police." I pressed the release buzzer to unlock the door and felt the blood drain out of my body. Something had happened to Kelly. An accident! "No, please God..."

I rushed to the bedroom, threw on a dressing gown and opened the front door to the apartment. Standing on the other side of the heavy metal security door were three people – a heavy set woman in pink slacks and white cardigan and two burly looking men in plain clothes. Without waiting to be asked inside they pushed past me and one of them closed my door. I stood staring, unable to speak. I did not want to hear that anything had happened to my child.

Then the woman spoke, "Mrs Grant, you are under arrest. Get dressed and come with us." Stunned into disbelief I sank onto the couch. "What do you mean arrest? Is this some sick joke – is this more intimidation from my husband?"

With a smile in her voice but not in her ice-cold eyes she said, "Yes, this is from your husband. He has laid charges of fraud against you."

"But what have I done!" I almost screamed. "What grounds have you got for this?"

The two men, in the meantime, were making themselves at home in my apartment. Walking around, examining the telephone, answering machine and casting sidelong glances at me.

I noticed the manila folder that the woman had carelessly tossed on the dining room table and asked to see what was in it. She put her hand on top of it. "Get dressed, we don't have all day."

I started feeling angry. The anger welled up in me like a volcano. "You cannot do this to me. I have rights. I am not going anywhere without my attorney."

"You can phone your attorney, but I don't have to give you any details."

With shaking fingers I dialled Leon's home number. "Leon, this is madness, I have three people here who say they are from the police and that I am under arrest!"

"What? Let me speak to one of them!"

I handed the phone to the aggressive woman and walked to

my bedroom. I threw on the first pair of slacks I could find and grabbed a light linen jacket. Without any makeup and with wet hair I walked back into the lounge and picked up the phone, ignoring them. Once again I dialled Leon's number.

"Verryn, go with them, I will meet you at the court. Don't say anything to them. Just co-operate. This is a set up."

I phoned my youngest brother, David, who lived about 10 kilometres from me. Haltingly I told him what was happening to me and asked him to come immediately.

"I'll be there now – don't move without me."

"Are you ready, Mrs Grant? "The sneering voice from the dark-haired man made my blood curdle. This was the voice of authority and he was enjoying every minute of this. "We need to get you to court, you know..." The thick Afrikaans accent sounded hollow in the tunnel, which had become my hearing and my vision.

"My brother is on his way. I am not going anywhere without him." I stared hard at him. He gazed back, looking me up and down, taking in the sopping wet hair and again, I saw that sneering grin.

Within 10 minutes David was at the door and he was confronted by three officious keepers of the law in the New South Africa. These three were still from the old school, the remaining dregs of the Afrikaner regime – they had no respect for the New Constitution and Human Rights. They were holding onto their jobs by the skin of their teeth and still believed that they had those unlimited powers of the previous government. Due to them, Trevor could continue to boast that money buys everything – even an unlawful arrest.

With barely controlled anger and gritted teeth David exploded, "What is going on here!"

"Where do you intend taking her?" Turning to me "Have they shown you any ID?"

Too numb to talk I shook my head.

The other man, smaller in stature than the aggressive one, hauled out an ID card and gave it to David.

"Has she been read her rights?" David towered over the cop.

"I'm sure Sonja read her the rights." He shrugged and turned away. "Let's go, it's getting late. We don't get paid overtime you know... Not like you rich okes, jy weet." The other two laughed at his feeble joke.

We got into the lift and David insisted that they allow me to drive with him in his Landcruiser. Sonja refused point blank. "You can follow us – she comes with us." They led me to the white Opel parked outside and the younger cop got into the backseat beside me. Sonja drove, the burly cop played with the radio.

She drove to the local police station where the burly one got out. Saying his goodbyes, the subtle innuendo was not lost on me, "Hope some of us have a good weekend." Suddenly, I realised that this was the long weekend, four days. Friday and Monday were public holidays. My heart started racing, they could lock me up for the long weekend – Oh dear God, what now?

I knew that the cops still had unlimited powers and with Trevor's vast wealth anything could be possible. I had no doubt that he had arranged this stunt and this was teaching me the ultimate lesson. With a sickening dread welling in me I realised in what a serious position I was. He didn't have to harass me or threaten my life; he had told me that he was going to frame me. I should have heeded his warning.

I must have been praying out loud. "Please God, help me, don't let this be happening to me. Please!"

As if she could read my mind Sonja turned to the rear, "Remove any valuable jewellery before we get to the courts.

Give it to your brother for safekeeping."

"Why? What is going to happen next? Where are you taking me?"

"We are taking you in for fingerprinting and official charging and then down to the court. Hopefully, if we can get a slot before a magistrate and your lawyer can apply for bail, you won't go to jail for the weekend." She put the car in gear and faced forward.

Frantically searching for David's car behind us, I sobbed uncontrollably. He was following closely and I shut my eyes wishing that I would die.

It seemed like days, months, years. I was out of touch with reality. My mind refused to function. I was as spaced out as I would ever be. I got out of the car when told to do so and fell into my brother's arms. He held me up forcing me to walk. Half carrying me into the dark brown brick building I clung to him, stumbling along. My senses suddenly returned and I could see every crack, every bit of graffiti and the filth. I could smell the musty smell as we were led down a long, dark passage. The building seemed to echo with hollow voices and the dampness felt like it was penetrating my skin.

We followed Sonja up two flights of stairs. Once cream walls were now stained and grey. The wooden banisters chipped and damaged. The rotten carpet tripping us as we lurched upwards.

David never relinquished his hold on me. "Be strong my girl. I won't leave you."

The male cop brought up the rear, whistling a monotonous tune.

We stopped before a door inset with a frosted glass panel. Mrs Authority unlocked the door and motioned us to sit on the green plastic chairs.

"This is not intimidation, David. This is a nightmare. It's horrendous! How does he get away with it?"

I was shouting. "This is not merely teaching me a lesson, David, he is going to destroy me, please help me..." I covered my face with my hands and sobbed and sobbed.

No one ever got the better of the self-proclaimed 'King of Bedfordview'. He had the money and money buys power. He had often told me that he could 'buy' lawyers, cops, doctors, judges, accountants, you name it.

Inside her office, Sonja seemed even more powerful and intimidating. The dark wooden desk was pocked with scratches and cigarette burns. Strewn with papers, it seemed to hold the key to a thousand heartaches.

With her official rubber stamp taking pride of place on her untidy desk, this woman wielded her power in no uncertain terms. My body was enveloped in an aura of hopelessness and fear. Thick, black fear. I could taste it.

I felt the cracked plastic on the green chair digging into my thigh. With a shuddering feeling of knowing I could sense the other souls who had sat in that very chair, uncertain as to where they were going to end up.

Both black and white South Africans had sat here and waited, with fear as their shadow, waiting for officialdom to proclaim their fate. How many innocent people had sat there wondering how they came to be there in the first place. Instinctively, I felt myself floating as part of a group. This had happened before and it would happen again. Only when the new government had rid themselves of the callousness and the righteousness of the previous regime would human rights take preference in this country.

I felt total compassion for all those people caught up in the struggle and felt a deep sense of shame welling up in me. I had been privileged. I had never become involved in political arenas – my life was too comfortable. I had covered my conscience by proclaiming that it was not my generation that had created the chaos and destruction of South Africa. I personally had never been racialist, so why was I to be involved? How wrong and selfish. I was to learn this lesson too late.

How many times had I read in the newspaper of people being arrested, locked up, held without charges, all in the name of state security. Now I was finding out that anyone could suffer the same consequences but for different reasons.

Sonja broke into my reverie and pushed a form across the desk. "Sign where marked X", blunt and to the point. What point? "What is this, what am I signing?"

Irritable sigh, "Read it, it's got your details, etc." David snatched it from me. Reading swiftly he threw the paper across the desk. "What are the charges?"

"We are investigating them and are still finding evidence." She gave David a steely look.

"How can you arrest someone before you have completed your investigation!" He leaned over the desk, putting his face right in front of hers. "Surely this country is not that backward?" My brother was becoming increasingly frustrated and she was starting to get angry.

I could see the pulse throbbing in David's cheek and knew that he was trying hard to control his temper.

She picked up the phone and asked for a constable to come through. "You will be taken for fingerprinting Ma'am," a sarcastic smile on her face. How much pleasure she took in watching the degradation of this haughty businesswoman who obviously enjoyed the good things in life. My very existence and background was counting heavily against me, let alone what I was supposedly guilty of.

I felt numb, a sense of dreaming enveloped me and when David pulled me to my feet I allowed him to steer me in the direction the young constable was indicating. I was floating in a sea of unreality and the room would not come back into focus.

"I am going to take fingerprints Ma'am, it will be a bit messy but I will help you wash it off." He was incredibly gentle. His young face swam into focus and for the first time I smiled. He deserved politeness, he was treating me like a human!

With leaden arms I held my hands up, first the left and then the right. The young cop did his duty. My fingers were covered in thick black ink. I was fascinated and held them up, staring at the lines on my thumbs. This was the first time I had taken notice of the patterns on my fingers, swirls and lines. Was this like the trunk of a tree? Was my life etched into the swirls? I was hypnotised and almost pulled away when the cop pushed my hands down and asked me to follow him to the basin.

David pushed me towards the basin. My legs were not working. My mind was elsewhere. I had taken the easy road out. I had absconded with my mind and left my body to do the dirty work. The policeman poured a thick, foul smelling liquid into my hands and placed a sponge on the side of the basin. With utmost gentleness, my brother, now realising how fragile my state of mind was, tears running down his own cheeks, scrubbed my hands and dried them on the filthy grey towel hanging over the basin, left there by the previous person who had been subjected to this act of belittlement.

Suddenly I came back to earth and with utmost clarity I knew where I was and what my situation involved. Officially now, I was a criminal. I had fingerprints on record and the South African Police were in control. Now they could throw the book at me. It was up to me to defend myself, no matter the cost.

Viva Trevor!

Mechanically, I followed the constable back towards Sonja's office. And once again sat on the cracked plastic chair. Now I was beyond all caring. I wanted to phone Michael and see how he was doing.

Taking out my cell phone and ignoring the quick look Mrs Authority gave me, I dialled the clinic. The switchboard operator put me through to the ward sister. She told me that Michael's condition had deteriorated and he was back in Intensive Care.

Sonja abruptly got up, signalling for us to follow her. David and I followed her and I remember the swish, swish of her slacks as her legs rubbed together. The other cop (the one from the arrest) materialised as from nowhere and took up the rear. As we walked out of the dismal building into the busy downtown Johannesburg street I looked around in amazement.

I had not been into Johannesburg city for about nine years. It had become far too dangerous and there was no need to enter the city. Most businesses had left the CBD and moved to the suburbs; it was safer and cleaner. The city had become a hawker's paradise. They were everywhere and they sold anything from apples to car tyres. Makeshift stalls with leaning tables overloaded with produce blocked the way for pedestrians who resignedly walked off the pavement and into the street to proceed on their way.

In a haze of new discovery I saw the faces of people. They were a motley bunch – hawkers, muggers, taxi warlords, potential hijackers – they were all milling around. These black faces, normally so intimidating for a white South African, now seemed so innocent and even comforting in a way. The threat to me was the two white faces which had dominated my vision this day. I made eye contact with one or two of them.

They were well aware of the police – these two stuck out like sore thumbs. I saw compassion in one of the faces – a silent message of hope. His eyes seemed to say, "Been there, done that, got the T shirt."

How many of these faces in the crowd, going about their own business, had at some time been subjected to the harsh attitude of the law in this country? The New Constitution advocated human rights. What had happened to me that morning had transgressed every rule in the book. A vindictive husband goes to the police, lays charges of fraud against his wife. The cops take his statement, don't investigate the so-called charges. They arrest the wife and in the process destroy her life. Husband walks around with another scalp hanging from his trophy belt. Only in South Africa could this happen at this time of change. Where was the system of justice?

Sonja insisted that I travel with her and told David to follow. The male detective, let's call him Piet (a common name in South Africa), accompanied us. He was there, I presume, to stop me escaping. As we drove down the crowded streets of Johannesburg I marvelled at the change. The city had once been a sophisticated metropolis, clean and buzzing.

Now it was congested with minibus taxis, hooters blaring. Fighting for their custom, the aggressive taxi drivers swerved in and out of lanes trying to get to the signalling pedestrians before their opposition could. The streets were littered and filthy. The hawkers I had seen earlier were mirrored by hundreds more. I saw stalls with pots and pans, kitchen cabinets, tools, you name it. Trading was brisk. Stall owners were conducting animated discussions with their customers. The African people are good traders and their people support them.

Drifters, hobos and street children interspersed with the busy buyers and sellers. Suspicious looking tsotsis were sauntering idly, keeping a beady eye open for that opportunity to mug an unsuspecting victim and make a dash for the next moment of financial security.

We arrived at the Johannesburg Magistrate's Court at 10.30 a.m. This ordeal had taken four and a half hours – I felt like my life had whizzed away and I was now at the very end.

As I walked into that courtroom my mind focussed on one thing only; to get myself out of there as quickly as possible. I saw my lawyer in front of me and went into robotic mode. I listened to everything he said, nodding my head. They made me sit on a bench lining the wall of the court. The high wooden platform where the magistrate would sit was looming over me like Table Mountain – just not as pretty or spiritually enlivening.

I do not remember what I said or what the magistrate said. I automatically answered questions, took the oath and stepped down when told to do so. Leon told me afterwards that I was terrific! He said the magistrate asked me if I knew why I was being charged. I apparently answered, "No, I don't. All I know is that my husband threatened to frame me and he has done so."

As I walked out of that building the seriousness of the situation eluded me. David had paid the bail of R30,000 ($7,500). Leon had the receipt in his file – an empty file. He had tried to get documentation or facts from Sonja and the prosecutor. They had nothing to give him. The matter was 'under investigation'.

I had been charged with fraud – the amount supposed to be over R500,000 ($125,000) and we still did not know how I was supposed to have perpetrated it. Leon was flabbergasted that they had managed to bring this issue in front of a magistrate with no supporting evidence and he was totally confused as to why this matter had been brought to the Magistrate's Court. By all accounts it should have been taken to the Supreme Court.

There were many, many grey areas and he was going to call in a senior advocate for counselling.

At Leon's request we crossed the road to a seedy little restaurant called 'Frangipani'. A more incongruous name could not be imagined. We sat down at a table decked with a brightly coloured plastic tablecloth and ordered coffees from the young man waiting on us.

Leon fired off a barrage at questions. I answered them to the best of my scattered memory. I had blocked out many moments that morning. David filled in as best he could. Piecing together the story he sat back in his chair. "This is going to make legal history. You were arrested on the grounds that your husband brought fraud charges against you. You were *never* questioned about his allegations. They were not investigated and authenticated. You were taken to the Magistrate's Court and charged. The amount is over R500,000. Strictly speaking no bail should have been allowed and yet they allowed bail. Under normal circumstances you would have been detained over the long weekend awaiting a formal application for bail." He was ticking these steps off on his fingers.

"This whole business was a set up and someone chickened out at the last minute. We have a clear case of wrongful and malicious arrest and we should sue the State for damages."

We arranged to meet on Tuesday morning 8 a.m. at his offices.

We drank our coffees, wished each other a good weekend and David and I drove out of Johannesburg.

I asked him to take me directly to the clinic. I wanted to see Michael urgently. I knew something was wrong. I had felt his presence from about 10.30 when we left Sonja's office.

CHAPTER TWENTY-ONE

The Avid Aviator

David dropped me at the clinic telling me he would pick me up in two hours' time. I hugged this darling brother of mine. "Thank you a million times for what you did for me this morning. I love you."

He gently disentangled himself from my bear hugs and said goodbye. I turned to wave at him, suddenly feeling that I didn't want to go into the clinic. A heavy sense of foreboding had descended on me and I did not want to be alone. He pulled out of the parking area and I walked slowly towards the entrance.

I went through the swing doors, down the passage and turned left for ICU. Mechanically I instructed my legs, my mind suddenly blank again. The ICU desk was unmanned. I stood there for some time in a haze of uncertainty trying to gather my thoughts.

"Excuse me sister, do you know where Mr Brent is?" She was in a hurry; an emergency bell was ringing somewhere. She looked at me blankly, and then realisation dawned. "Wait here, I'll be back now."

A minute later she returned with another nurse. I knew this one. She had been on duty the day before. I saw the look of evasiveness on her face. "Where is Michael?" Panic welling up in my chest. She picked up the desk phone and spoke quietly. The senior sister on duty, who I had also met before, materialised as if she was the genie in the lamp.

Taking my arm she led me into an adjoining ward and sat me in a chair. "Mrs Grant, I'm sorry... we have already contacted his ex-wife in Portugal and we have spoken to Gavin Mulder..."

She was babbling and my patience wore thin. "What are you talking about – I want to see Michael NOW!"

"You don't understand, I'm sorry, Mr Brent passed away this morning at 10.30."

I woke up in one of the wards. I was lying fully clothed under a white blanket. My dear friend Kate was sitting next to the bed. She was holding my hand. Sitting bolt upright I started crying, full realisation hitting me like a ton of bricks.

"Kate, Michael is dead! I need to see him. Where have they taken him?"

Gently she helped me off the high bed and straightened my clothes. Tears were streaming down her face. She found my shoes and helped me put them on and rang the bell for the sister.

The nursing sister swept into the room holding a glass of water and a tablet. I knew instinctively that if I did not take the tablet she would not let me see Michael. I obeyed, swallowing fast.

Silently, she led Kate and I down the passage to the lift. No one uttered a word as we rode up to the top floor. I was ice cold and shivering. It was steaming hot outside.

The lift opened into a foyer with double glass doors leading off to both sides. Sterile white and nothing else. Hospital heaven. So quiet, so deathly. We went through the door on the left. No one had to direct me. I knew instinctively which door it was.

The hospital trolley was against the wall covered with a white sheet. The room was icy cold. The air conditioner was turned up to the coldest temperature, no doubt. I stood, teeth chattering, in the centre of the room. Turning to Kate I asked her and the sister to leave. "I would like to be left alone with him – please?"

I could not share this with any other person, no matter how dear they were to me.

It was quiet, the hum of the aircon fading into the stillness. I stood staring at the trolley waiting for movement. He would, any minute now, move his foot. I could see the shape of it so clearly, angled to the left.

I closed my eyes willing him to wake up and talk to me. "Michael, I have to tell you what happened to me today. It is like a fairy story. It's about a wicked monster and a Jack in the Beanstalk Giant. Do you want to hear it?"

After a thousand years I walked slowly towards the white sheet and lifted the top end. Michael's eyes were closed; his eyelashes pitch black, touching his cheeks. His mouth was set in a perfect shape, relaxed and on the brink of a smile. His forehead was uncreased. He looked so young and carefree. His skin had lost the pallor I had become accustomed to in the last few days. It had returned to its former healthy glow.

I stared and stared. He looked so healthy, so young, so alive, so asleep. Perhaps I should leave him to sleep, he would wake up feeling better...

I leaned over and kissed his lips like I used to when he was downstairs. He would stir and wake up, sleepy eyed.

I smelled the sterile lotion and pulled back, cold fact dawning on a numb brain.

I pulled the sheet down and saw his folded arms. I put my hands over his and clasped them tight. They were cold and soft. So very soft. Too frail for my Michael. So very white, his nails showing a bright hue of pink. I stood there stroking his hands and touching his nails, tears drowning me so that I could no longer see his body. I was blinded and needed to touch him. His chest felt cold and the curly black hair was gooey with a gel or lotion. I looked for a cloth so that I could wipe him. In the corner was a basin with a white towel draped on the side. I wet half of it and started wiping his face.

The door opened and the sister came in. She saw what I was doing and took the towel away, not saying a word. Kate came in carrying a chair and placed it next to the trolley. "Sit here, Verryn, say your goodbyes. They are not going to allow you much more time." She walked out of the room.

I don't remember what I said to Michael. Kate told me that I had spoken for about half an hour. When she came in I had my head on his chest and I looked as if I was sleeping. She led me from the room and took me home to her house where she put me to bed.

CHAPTER TWENTY-TWO

Farewell coming

The funeral home was located on the hill in Braamfontein, just 2 kilometres outside of the Johannesburg city centre. The area, once an upmarket CBD, had degenerated into a skeleton suburb. Most businesses had relocated to the northern suburbs where their customers and staff could come and go in relative safety. Although, the hijacking statistics indicated that Sandton, heart of the northern suburbs had a high risk factor.

Braamfontein had become home to drifters, muggers and car thieves. Normally, I would have been on the alert for any suspicious looking character and would have parked my car right outside of the entrance. That day, hijacking or mugging was a trifling thing compared to what I was suffering. I had to see Michael again.

It was Tuesday, the long weekend had passed in a blur of tears and fear. Grief for my Michael and fear of Trevor. Kate had taken me to the doctor on the Friday and he had given me a prescription for sleeping pills and tranquillisers. Ten of each. "Just enough to get you through this bad period." I looked at him and knew that he had not the slightest idea of how bad this period was. How long was this bad period going to last?

The funeral home was modern and impressive in architecture. It was known to be the most expensive and the best. The tall, dark man that was called to reception looked the part. He could not have looked more sombre and eerie. He was ever so helpful and solicitous. He offered me coffee and when I declined he led me downstairs. "This is the pause area for mourners. The viewing room is right here." He pointed to a heavy oak door. I stepped into the room and stopped in my tracks.

The amount of effort and thought that had gone into decorating Michael's room was quite breathtaking. His accountant and long time friend, Gavin, had followed instructions to the letter.

The room was decorated in 'Avid Aviator' style. Photos of Michael were mounted in decorator style. Photos of him in his little Cessna, in the Piper that eventually crashed in Namibia, the King Air, his little bi-plane called Monty, his Microlite, every aircraft that he had ever owned. His vast collection of little planes was displayed in the centre of the room.

I stood in the doorway breathing in the essence of this man who had stolen my heart and had flown away. This was reality, so real, we were indeed saying goodbye to the Avid Aviator.

The Kiaat coffin, to side of the room, was mounted on an exquisitely carved trestle table. No glass and chrome and red velvet for this man, never! I was positive that the table came from the game farm and knew that either Vusi or Philemon had carved it. Perhaps they had shared this labour of love.

I moved closer, expecting to see only Michael's face, shrouded in white. Flashbacks of my father's funeral were echoing in my mind. I was wrong. I stared in awe at my beloved darling.

He was dressed in a pure cotton shirt that I had given him for his birthday the year before. It was patterned in muted colours of grey, green, blue and cream. He used to love it. He said it reminded him of the colours of the veld. On the pocket the little logo seemed to shine irridescent as if it held a life force of it's own.

I reached down to touch it and felt the hardness of an object in the pocket. I knew what it was before I could trace the outline with my finger.

How many months, days, years ago had I given Michael the little pewter eagle? I had picked it up at a flea market stall in the Natal Midlands and had known immediately that it was made for him. Probably the cheapest gift he had ever received. He had treasured it. He carried it in his wallet for good luck and would not fly without it. Countless times, either in the bush, or in a pub, or at his home, I had seen him take it out of the wallet and hold it gently. He had gone so far as to have it copied onto the side of the King Air plane and that plane was named 'Flight of the Eagle'.

I knew, without a measure of doubt, that Michael had clinically organised his funeral and every aspect of his death. Even in death people would follow his instructions and be led by the strong memory of him. He would not be forgotten easily.

I stood there stroking the eagle and the strangest thing happened. I don't know if I dreamed it or if it was real – I think it could have been real. From my fingertips, right up my arm there was a burning sensation. It carried on into my chest and I stood there absorbing the aura of this man, taking strength from him and understanding the silent message being relayed to me.

I stared at the face that I had loved so deeply and saw that the peace and tranquillity of Michael had been born. No longer was he troubled and angry at the world. His face had settled into the look of someone in a deep sleep. His mouth was no longer on the brink of a smile but was composed and fuller than I had seen it for a long time. His eyebrows seemed so heavy and those long eyelashes thicker and blacker than ever.

They had combed his hair wrong. He never wore a parting. His hair had a natural growth pattern and was always swept back. I made a mental note to tell the sombre man.

I leaned over and kissed those lips again. The strange smell and the coldness of his lips did not frighten me. I whispered to him, saying those special things that we had made up.

I became aware of other people in the room and recognised a couple who had done business with Michael. He had helped them start their own business, which was prospering. No doubt they wanted to say thank you to their mentor. Two of many, many people who had been helped by Michael's kindness.

I greeted them, slipped quietly out of the room and drove home to experience the pain of loss in private.

CHAPTER TWENTY THREE

The ex-wife returns

The call came late at night. "Hi Verryn, it's me, Linda, How are you?"

"I'm fine thanks, Linda. When did you arrive?"

"Oh, early this evening. Came for the funeral..." The voice broke and I held on while she tried to compose herself. "Can you come and fetch me? I don't want to be by myself." Now I could hear that she was more than a little drunk.

With a sinking feeling I knew that I would have to go to her and perhaps bring her home to the apartment. It was nearly midnight and I had already taken a sleeping tablet. Besides, my brain was telling me that it was too dangerous to travel that late at night. "Where are you Linda?"

"At the Belvedere, not far from you." Thank goodness. This was a hotel apartment block only recently completed and within five kilometres. Still, the threat of hijacking made me hesitate. A woman on her own late at night was an easy target and I was groggy from the tablet. She sensed my reluctance.

"Please Verryn, I can't stay on my own. Michael is dead and I don't know what to do!"

"I'll be there now." Hastily I put on a tracksuit and drank a glass of coca cola.

The apartment building was garishly lit up. I got there in record time, not stopping at red lights, just checking for other traffic and going through.

The guard at the gate was sleeping in his little glass cubicle. When my headlights shone on him, he jumped up and staggered to the window thrusting his logbook at me. I filled in my name and car registration and Linda's name as the person to be visited. He took ages to look at his listing and find which unit Linda was in. Eventually, he sighed, "Mrs Da Silva is in Block A unit 12. He pushed the remote control button and the heavy metal gates opened slowly. He waved me through and I parked outside the first block.

She took ages to answer the door. I was dreading that she had passed out and I had come in vain.

She opened the door after many rings. Dishevelled hair, makeup smeared, eyes red. She was very drunk.

She put her arms around me and I shrank from the stale alcohol smell. The apartment was chaotic, clothes and papers everywhere. There were empty wine glasses and a bottle on the coffee table.

She sat down on the couch. "Pour me a drink please, Verry. Have one yourself..." The abbreviation of my name irritated me. "No thanks, Linda and I don't think you should have any more either. It's past midnight."

The watery blue eyes filled. I watched as the tears plopped out of her eyes and felt helpless. How could I console her? I did not know the extent of her feelings and I had never been close to her. She wasn't even a friend. I was shocked when she started speaking. Incoherently at first but as the sorry tale of guilt and lost love poured out I felt deep empathy with her. Michael had been right. She was helpless and could never really take care of herself. Her new husband, left behind in Portugal, was a playboy who never took responsibility – that's what the rumour was.

Her story started to make sense. She missed Michael and felt guilty because she had run off with Luis. She blamed herself for hurting Michael. The contradictions of emotion and repetitiveness seemed never ending.

I let her talk for ages and then started telling her how deeply Michael cared for her. "Linda, don't blame yourself for everything. Michael never blamed you for going with Luis. He wanted you to be happy."

The sudden change in mood took me by surprise. She reached over, poured the remains of the wine into one of the dirty glasses. Taking a gulp and staring at me with defiant eyes. "I always hated you. You were the woman that Michael wanted. From the first time he set eyes on you. He was fascinated."

I got up, anticipating one of those scenes she was known for. I did not need this at one o'clock in the morning. "NO, don't go! You sit down and listen to me! He never stopped talking about you. You are a wonderful mother, an excellent businesswoman, always well groomed, a model of a wife, all the shit in the world!" She took another drink of wine. "I always thought differently – I could not stand your mode of perfection."

My mind was reeling. Michael and I had never spent time together whilst he was married to Linda. The only times we spent together was in social groups. Except for the incident in Botswana we had never transgressed the boundaries of our commitments to our partners. He remained faithful to Linda for months after she had run off with Luis. Shrugging my shoulders I decided that there was no point in trying to convince her.

"You don't have to believe me but your husband was devastated when you left him. He became a recluse for nearly a year and locked himself up in the house or spent many lonely hours at Falcon's Rest. Think what you like, I'm going home."

She reached over, grasping my hand. "Please don't leave me here. I'm sorry for what I just said. You are a true friend. Be my friend, please..."

After I had put Linda to bed I sat on the uncomfortable

couch wondering whether I should let myself out and go home or whether I should just lie down and sleep for a while. The sleeping pill was wearing off and I didn't feel that I would sleep that easily. I closed my eyes and started thinking about her words. I always knew that she loved Michael deeply. Why she left him I could never fathom, but there must have been some emotional scarring from the abortion that had caused her to want to hurt him so much. Michael was the kind of man that once married, never divorced and never stopped protecting – even after divorce and yes, right beyond death. He would still look after her. How could she be so insecure?

I dozed off and some two hours later woke with a start, not knowing where I was and for an awful moment thinking that Trevor had done something to me and I was locked up in a strange place. With a pounding heart I felt a wave of absolute terror wash over me.

I had not given much thought to the court event as my attorneys were now 'looking into the matter.' I had been so drained with Michael's passing that the seriousness of this issue still eluded me. Perhaps it was due to the fact that I had lived a sheltered life and did not really understand the sordidness and vindictiveness of Trevor's world.

Looking at my watch I saw that it was after 6 a.m. and I needed to get home and shower and start contacting the lawyers. I woke Linda and offered her a cup of coffee.

She opened those pale blue eyes awash with hangover hues and stared non-plussed.

"What are you doing here?"

"Linda, you phoned me last night and I came over to be with you – I slept on the couch but I am leaving here soon – are you okay to get through the day?"

"No, I have to come with you, I have no transport. Please Verryn, don't leave me on my own, you know what will happen..." She tried some emotional blackmail. "...I'll just drink and drink."

She paused, then pleaded, "Please take me to see Michael – I have to see him."

We left my apartment at 10.30 a.m. and headed for Braamfontein. This would be my second visit to the funeral home and I was not looking forward to Linda's hysterics.

I tried to instill a sense of calm into her as we drove and offered her lunch afterwards, which she immediately accepted. As we drove the announcer on the radio called the next song and with a ball of lead in my tummy I hummed along to the words that Michael and I played and sang so often. They were written for us and we adapted them into a language of our own. It was if he had orchestrated the song to be played right then, to tell me that I would be all right and that he loved me still. I tried to imagine that he was talking to both of us – the two women in his life – and felt that I was sharing this sentiment with Linda. She, however, had her head back and eyes closed, heavy framed dark glasses hiding her puffy eyes.

The sombre, dark man was on duty again, he recognised me and once again offered his marketing hospitality, which we declined. As we were ushered into the viewing room I saw that the trestles were not holding their precious cargo. With a sad smile, the dark man said, "I'll just arrange for the dearly departed to be brought through."

With horror I realised that there must be some form of cold storage where the bodies were kept and shuddered. Michael would be so cold in there; he always felt the cold and loved his open log fires.

I began feeling nauseous and wanted to leave but Linda was holding my hand so tightly that I had trouble walking straight. With trepidation I waited for the hysterics to start and I was not wrong.

As they wheeled a trolley with the magnificent coffin into the room, she started sobbing and held her hands in front of her face, refusing to look at him. She was babbling incoherently a mixture of love and recrimination. It was confusing and frightening to hear. I put my arms around her and led her to the leather couch, pushed her down and rang the bell for coffee. Linda scrabbled in her handbag, found a pillbox and popped a small pink tablet into her mouth.

I got up and walked over to Michael and touched his face. He was ice cold and his hair felt sticky. Now I started dry retching and walked from the room. Blindly following the arrows I reached the toilet just in time.

Standing with my forehead against the cold tiles in the basin area, I tried to calm down and carry on with this charade. For me it was a charade, I could not give vent to my feelings in front of this woman. We were adversaries, not friends and she was screwed up. I did not have the emotional strength to cope with this. Rinsing my mouth and trying to calm down as best I could, I looked in the mirror and saw how haggard and stressed I looked. God, this was not me, not the bouyant Verryn who could face any challenge.

Getting Linda out of the building was easy; the prospect of lunch and cold wine made it so. As we drove into the restaurant car park, she took out her lipstick and fluffed out her blonde hair. I parked the BMW next to a new Mercedes, which had just pulled in before us, and as I got out I saw the passenger in the front seat turn towards us and wave. Looking at Linda I saw her reciprocate and flash him a dazzling smile.

"Who is that, Linda?"

"Oh, don't you know John Slabbert. He used to do business with Michael."

The tall, grey-haired man was now waiting for us to walk down the brick pathway and I noticed the exaggerated swagger in Linda's step. We made the usual introductory noises and proceeded into the foyer.

The manageress, whom I knew quite well, took up two menus and led us to a table in the bay window overlooking the duck pond. Linda took the chair facing into the restaurant and I sat down facing the window. The waitress brought the wine list and Linda chose without even looking. She favoured a Semillon and any brand would do. She lifted her handbag and took out a packet of cigarettes. I was taken aback as I could not remember her ever smoking.

She must have seen my look of surprise because she volunteered the information. "I started smoking again after I married Luis. He smokes a lot and I decided that I might as well join him instead of putting up with the bad breath – garlic and nicotine! I used to smoke when Michael and I were courting but I gave it up when we adopted the baby." A stern look passed over her face and she leaned forward, "You know about the baby don't you? Michael would have told you, I know." I nodded, not feeling that words would make the situation any better.

"I guess he did not tell you the full story, in fact, I am prepared to bet on that!"

"What would you like to eat, Linda?"

I tried to change the subject but failed dismally.

"Don't skirt the issue, Verryn, did he tell you the whole story, yes or no?"

"I don't know what you mean Linda, and I am not concerned about the whole story as you put it. That was your history with Michael, keep it sacred."

"No, Verryn, you also built up history with him and you should know about mine."

The waitress interrupted us and opened the bottle of chilled wine. We ordered our food and lifted our glasses in a silent toast. Linda took a few big gulps and refilled her glass before the waitress could do her duty. I sat back and tried to relax. My mind was churning with the queries I needed to sort out with my lawyer that evening at 6 p.m.

After the third glass of wine, Linda pushed back her chair and lit another cigarette.

"So, my dear, how is your divorce going, I hear Trevor is being particularly nasty."

Never surprised at the power of the Bedfordview grapevine, I took it for granted that she was well informed as to my situation. However, I liked to believe that no one knew about his latest act of intimidation. This was my secret and I was so humiliated by it. If I had not had the distraction of Michael's death, I would have been totally destroyed by what had happened. Yet now I had more important things to worry about. The forthcoming memorial service, the cremation, scattering his ashes, etc. All these things needed thinking about. My problems could wait for a week.

I decided to change the subject and asked Linda if she wanted to say a few words at the memorial service. Michael had not been to church for many years and had requested that his funeral service be non-religious and simple. His close friend and accountant, Gavin, had already asked me to prepare a farewell speech and I was going to keep it brief.

"No thanks, I wouldn't know what to say, being the ex-wife and all. I am considered persona non grata and they can all go to hell as far as I'm concerned."

I knew that this was the beginning of one of those characteristic 'Linda scenes' and was powerless to stop it.

Taking a long pull on her cigarette, she closed her eyes as she exhaled and leaned forward. I stared at the bulging cleavage and withheld a shudder. How could he have been married to this woman?

"Michael used to hit me, you know..." The emphasis on the word made my stomach turn.

My breath caught in my throat and I turned to get u. "Excuse me, I have to go to the toilet." I almost ran to the toilet and once inside started breathing again. I could not endure another five minutes with this woman; she stressed me enormously. I did not want to hear her talking about Michael and I did not believe he did awful things to her. Michael was strong, caring, protective and powerful. He always looked after her. How ungrateful she was being.

I knew that she accepted that Michael and I had had a close and caring relationship, more friends than lovers. Most of our social circle thought of it that way. Of course, there was speculation but then in our circle there was always speculation and scandal. Even I did not know how to classify our relationship. What had we been? I knew that I loved him deeply but I was so confused as to what his emotions had been. My only consolation was that he had told me so many times that he loved me and did not want to hurt me. Why was he so fanatical about hurting me?

As I walked back to the table I saw that it was empty and then, looking around, I saw Linda sitting at the table with John and the man he had arrived with. She waved and I walked over in trepidation. They had ordered liqueurs and she was swigging hers back with gusto. "Sit down, lovely lady, and have a drink." The red-faced, paunchy Mercedes owner pulled out the spare chair and patted it. "No thanks, I think I am going to leave now. Linda are you ready?" I knew before she answered. "No thanks dear, John will be taking me home. You go on and I'll speak to you on the phone." I left her in the care of the two half inebriated men and walked out of the restaurant promising myself that I would not worry about her again.

CHAPTER TWENTY-FOUR

The legal battle begins

The drive to Pretoria was hectic, the main road was extremely busy and no one stuck to the speed limit. You either drove at their pace or became intimidated by flashing lights and rude signs. The business sector was on its way home and the day in the city had been enough to turn the most docile creature into a raving lunatic. Living with the constant fear of hijacking, mugging, robbing, murder and listening to the radio brought more doom and gloom. People in this country were living on the edge all the time.

I parked as close to the building as I could, locked the car and rushed into the foyer clutching my bag and ran up two flights of stairs. This building did not have the customary security guard at the entrance and it would be too dangerous to get into one of the lifts.

As I sat in the waiting room I looked around at the people present. Every one of them looked unhappy and stressed. I assumed they were mostly divorce cases and each one of them knew that this was one of the most expensive lawyers in South Africa. I hoped that he would do the right thing for them. If only I had known then what an expensive trip this was going to be for me and how much abuse I was going to suffer at the hands of the legal profession in South Africa.

When my turn came I entered the plush office of the senior partner and said hello to the senior advocate and the junior advocate employed to hear the details of the latest form of harassment dished out by Trevor.

I had warned these two advocates in a previous meeting that Trevor had phoned me to say that he was going to frame me and stop me from ever going to Australia to be with my girls and they had done nothing about his threats. Now I was facing fraud charges and they were joking about the incident with absolute nonchalance.

"We will get the charges dropped but we need to get a criminal barrister as my partner is too slack – he doesn't act quick enough," my lawyer said.

I could not believe my ears. This well-known lawyer was telling me, his client, that his own partner was slack! Throughout this meeting my fears of what could happen to me were mounting and I was almost becoming hysterical. I broke down and cried, asking them for clear advice as to what I should do and what the next step was to be. They seemed oblivious to the trauma I had suffered in the Magistrate's Court and did not seem to understand what the stigma of an arrest would do to my children and me. I had not told Amber and Sarah. Kelly knew what had happened but not the extent of the trouble I was in.

At the end of that meeting I walked out of the office feeling as if my world had crumbled and I was alone with no idea of what to do next. None of these so-called high powered legal men had done anything to calm me down or reassure me. To them this was just another case and they were undoubtedly going to make big bucks out of it. By calling in more barristers and spreading the load and the financial gain they could feast on my sorrow.

I drove home oblivious of any dangers the dark winding road may have concealed. I was lost in a world of abject misery and frightened out of my wits.

As I entered the apartment I remembered that Kelly was spending the night at a friend's place and made straight for my bedroom. I undressed and sat down on the floor with the cupboard door open. The safe was bolted into the corner and I stared at it for ages. Slowly I pressed the combination numbers and the door swung open. I took out the Taurus 38 Special and held it in my hand.

I felt the smoothness of the glistening metal and remembered the last time I had used it at the practice range. It was a sensation of no return when you pulled that trigger and the power of the kick to your wrist as the bullet discharged was awesome. What release it seemed to hold. I put the gun down next to the bed and went into the study where I found writing paper and a pen. I wrote one letter, addressed to all three girls. I could never share those words with any other person but those three beautiful women. All my emotions and regrets were laid bare and I begged for their forgiveness. Folding the letter, sodden with my tears, I placed it in my bedside drawer.

I picked up the gun once more and sat on the floor cradling it to my chest, praying to Jesus to forgive me what I was about to do. Begging for the strength to hold it at an angle that would not slip and leave me a vegetable for life, I asked God to give me the strength to carry through with my wish to end my life.

I had never considered suicide as an option in my entire life. I had always been in control and always had the utmost faith in my personal strength of character to get me through any situation. This dilemma was bigger than the worst imaginable – this was a nightmare and I was not waking up from it.

Michael's death had numbed me to my own problems but each day the cold realisation of what I stood to face and the hopelessness of fighting a powerful man like Trevor made me want this way out. I had seen him rip people's lives apart with his vindictiveness and had often felt nauseated by his callousness but had always been powerless to intervene. I had heard of incidents that had made my blood chill but had chosen not to believe them. Now I knew that he was the cruellest man ever and that he would stop at nothing to destroy me. I was not wrong; Trevor's campaign of terror had only just started.

The intercom rang shrilly and disturbed my reverie. I froze; perhaps this was another policeman, perhaps it was Trevor – what should I do? Gripping the gun tightly I lifted it and held the cold barrel to my forehead.

The intercom rang continuously and then the telephone started ringing. I picked up the receiver and before I could say anything I heard my brother, Brian, saying, "It's me – I'm downstairs, let me in."

Hastily I pushed the gun under the bed and walked unsteadily into the hall to press the release buzzer for the lobby doors. I rushed to the bathroom and wiped my face before unlocking the door and the heavy iron security door to let my brother in. He put his arms around me and held me tightly for a long time. No words were necessary, this man had always been very psychic and he had known what I intended to do. He had arrived just in time to prevent this act of desperation.

We busied ourselves with making coffee in the tiny kitchen while I told him everything that had happened. With his jaw clenched he asked curt questions and made no comment as I poured out the tale of disgrace, shame and fear. He then went to the telephone and I heard him talking quietly, telling whomever it was, the story he had just heard. When he put the phone down I sat next to him on the couch, too tired to stand any longer and too weary to care about anything.

"I have asked a very good friend of mine to come over and see us tomorrow afternoon. He is an advocate and I think he may be able to help you more than your lawyers can. I think you have been neglected by your lawyer and I don't think he is going to be much good in getting you out of this situation."

"What can he do, more so than anyone else. Trevor's money can buy and bribe anything and anyone. I don't stand a chance. He wants to destroy me."

"Trevor is the meanest bastard I have ever come across. He cannot destroy you; we will fight him and give him a taste of his own medicine."

Hollow words. Only I knew what terrible acts Trevor was capable of and to what lengths he would go in order to get even. He thrived on revenge and got his kicks from seeing people broken. Haltingly, I started telling Brian about some of the evil deeds that I knew Trevor had been involved in and he listened intently. With the steaming mug of coffee held in my hands I recounted the following stories to my brother who listened with mounting anger and disbelief.

About 15 years previously, long before he and I were married, Trevor had enlisted the services of a company who employed undercover agents. He was experiencing stock losses in his warehouse and wanted to crack the ring that was operating internally. This company placed a skilled black man in the warehouse ostensibly as a packer but he was there to observe and report on any untoward happenings.

After a couple of weeks of observation this man submitted his report and the gang of thieves were trapped and charged with theft. Even in those days, it was difficult to dismiss an employee. Guilt or negligence had to be proved otherwise strike action by sympathetic co-workers was a dire threat.

The thieves were dismissed and the undercover agent 'resigned'. Shortly thereafter Trevor received a call from this man telling him that he wanted R20,000 ($5000) or he was going to inform all the 200 factory workers that management had enlisted the services of undercover agents (illegal in terms of the union laws) which would result in an immediate strike and cripple the business.

Trevor consulted with his contact in a gang that specialised in teaching people lessons they would never forget and they decided to deal with the blackmailer in their own fashion. Trevor agreed to their proposal and they set it in motion.

The man called again demanding the money and Trevor told him that he would arrange for a briefcase, containing the money, to be delivered to a remote spot near to a town some 110 kilometres away. The area they chose was dense bush and totally deserted. The blackmailer was ambushed when he came to pick up the briefcase, which contained paper sheets. The man who had tried his luck with the well known and self-styled King of Bedfordview was never seen again.

I wondered whether his wife or wives, as it is the custom for blacks to have more than one wife, ever tried to trace him and where their search ended. How many children had been left without desperately needed financial support? Was there any trace of this man's remains and would they ever be found and identified? At that time in South Africa, many thousands of black people went 'missing' and no effort was made to find them. The Afrikaner government had too many other important matters to spend money on.

Trevor used to tell the following story at many dinner parties and he was very proud of it.

John, a businessman who owned a small opposition company, had been making enquiries regarding the ethics of certain large contracts awarded to Trevor. Trevor phoned him and told him to back off or else! John was a self-made man who had done extremely well for himself yet kept his business small and profitable and wanted a fair chance at tendering for contracts. He was not into bribery or corruption and stood his ground.

John had recently bought himself a new Jaguar. One Friday night John and his wife dined at a restaurant in Sandton.

His Jaguar was parked under a huge oak tree in the dimly lit parking lot. When he and his wife strolled out into the summer night, having enjoyed company of close friends, they were not expecting what they saw. The Jaguar had been wrecked. No part of the bodywork was left without a dent, battery acid had been poured over the vehicle and every window was smashed. It was virtually unrecognisable.

John called the police and apparently voiced his suspicions as to who was responsible for the destruction. He reported to them that Trevor had threatened him with physical violence. He called a mutual friend of ours and told him that Trevor was hitting on him and that he was in fear of his life. Trevor was never questioned and John still tells everyone that Trevor organised the 'panel beating' of his new Jag.

Trevor openly boasted of his actions and feared no recourse. He had a reputation of being a man who was 'not to be crossed' and he lived up to his image with much aggression.

The next story, tame by comparison, made my brother even angrier.

We had been holidaying at the flat in Natal and it was New Year's Day some years before. We had driven back from Sarah's home in Durban where we had spent the previous night and as we pulled into the car park we saw that a red Toyota had parked in our bay. Trevor, at that time drove a Mercedes sports car. He parked his vehicle behind the Toyota, went inside and phoned a towing company to remove the offending vehicle.

When the tow personnel arrived they found that the vehicle was parked in gear and it could not be towed away without severely damaging the gearbox.

By this stage a number of holidaymakers in the complex were standing around watching Trevor give a show of importance. I had remained inside but Amber was outside and she tells the story of him saying at the top of his voice, "I paid a million Rand for my car and it has to stand in the sun whilst some piece of shit is parked in my bay. I don't stand for this kind of crap." With that he walked into the flat and got a hammer from the toolbox, walked outside and smashed the driver's window. He then yanked the door open, took the car out of gear and instructed the open-mouthed technicians to remove the vehicle immediately.

Strangely enough the owner of the vehicle was totally unaware of what was going on and only discovered that his car was missing the next morning. When he saw all the smashed glass he thought his car had been stolen and reported it to the police. Later that morning one of the other residents informed him that his vehicle had been towed away.

I received a phone call on my mobile. It was from a highly irate man who told me that my husband had damaged his son's vehicle and he was going to sue for compensation. I apologised to him, telling him that I did not witness the incident and that I was most embarrassed.

With that, he calmed down and said, "Mrs Grant, everyone in the complex is talking about your husband. He seems to be a fool. I am deeply sorry for you. You sound like a cultured lady, goodbye."

During the eight years I was married to Trevor I slowly became aware of how he operated. By his own description he was a 'wheeler dealer'. He had no conscience, no fear of authority, bribed anyone who stood in his way, destroyed lives by wreaking havoc and took revenge on anyone who tried to stand up to him. I used to cringe when I heard him ranting at people over the phone and never took his threats as serious. I thought he was past being a mafia type and viewed him as a bully at the age of 66.

I was sadly mistaken, Trevor had a huge network of contacts and he had cleverly worked out a system of intimidation so that he would always have a background of information on the person and could use this to blackmail them into doing what he wanted.

During our marriage I became aware of no less than 22 people of all ranks and stations that Trevor had 'investigated'. He had thick manila files stored in a wall safe detailing every aspect of their lives. He had employed teams of detectives to follow them, break into their homes and their businesses, gather documentation and photograph them at various activities, etc. He kept these files for 'insurance' and for 'when the time was right to play his hand'.

He knew most aspects of the law in South Africa and bragged that he employed different teams of lawyers and advocates to ensure that he always remained in the clear. The handful of people who had attempted to take him to court never succeeded in obtaining justice. In the meantime he manipulated and manoeuvred people out of their own businesses, destroying their livelihood and having no remorse for the break up of their family lives.

Trevor also had a longstanding relationship with a notorious gangster called Craven. At one stage they had both owned Ferraris and belonged to a sports car club. From the day they met they entered into an illegal diamond smuggling operation and their relationship was stormy and violent with death threats bandied back and forth.

I remember a phone conversation, with Trevor screaming at the other person that he was going to get them 'done in' and when he slammed the phone down he stormed out of the house, returning hours later. Some months later Craven died in a car accident somewhere in the Cape Province.

"My God, Verryn, when did you find out?" "How long have you known about these things?" my brother exclaimed.

"Not long. I have heard so much about Trevor's exploits in

the last few months. All the stories are coming out now that people know that we have split up."

"This guy is a monster. I hated him from the first time I met him. You are going to be harassed no end."

My brother put his mug down, walked to the window and drew the lounge curtains.

"Why haven't you employed a bodyguard this trip?"

"Because every cop in Bedfordview, and Johannesburg for that matter, knows about the previous incidents and my lawyers have threatened him with an interdict. I know that he is a coward. He is a bully and I willnot let his hate campaign impact on Kelly's life."

"He is a coward, we'll just make sure that he leaves you alone from now onwards. I am going to pay him a visit."

"Please don't get involved. I am leaving the country as soon as I get my passport back and then I'll be far away from his threats and bully boy actions."

"You look a wreck, Verryn. I'm going home now, or would you rather prefer that I stayed here tonight?"

"I'm okay. You go home, I'll take a sleeping pill and crash."

When Brian left I got into bed and pulled the duvet over my head. My body started shaking uncontrollably.

I felt ice cold. The thought of what could have happened left me shuddering. How could I allow Trevor to wreak the ultimate havoc in my life and those of my children? He would be in seventh heaven if I committed suicide. I prayed with all my heart for God to forgive me for what I had contemplated and begged for His guidance and protection.

I resolved to fight the fictitious charges and return to Australia as soon as I could.

CHAPTER TWENTY-FIVE

The funeral

Michael had told me that he wanted his funeral service to be held on Banghulele, the game preservation farm that he sponsored in Bronkhorstspruit, about 80 kilometres outside of Johannesburg. He chose this location, as he knew that it would be difficult for his many labourers and trusted employees from his game farm and other businesses to find transport and their way around the big city of Johannesburg.

He would have preferred the service to have been on his own game farm but that was too far for the 'city crowd' to travel, so this was the compromise.

For many years he had funded various projects on this preservation farm and had recently built a hippo enclosure for a rare albino species.

This farm also had a chapel built by a farmer who owned it almost 60 years ago. The chapel was built in honour of his wife who died in childbirth.

Michael had stipulated that he wanted a simple service (not 'heavy') and that he wanted to be cremated.

His ashes had to be strewn at the waterhole, deep in the African bush, on his own game farm at Falcon's Rest.

I drove slowly along the rutted road. I had left home at 5 a.m. so that I could drive into the sunrise and say my prayers as I drove. I often speak to God when I drive. It is the only time when I am really alone and can speak about my secrets and ask for guidance. The road from Johannesburg had been deserted and I had had a heartfelt conversation with God. I felt relaxed and peaceful and very close to Michael, almost as if he was sitting next to me in the car. I started talking to him, telling him about the wildflowers and in the distance I could see the herd of elephants donated to Banghulele. There were two adult cows and eight babies. The young ones came from all different parts of Africa and had been taken in at the farm for protection for various reasons. The two adult cows had adopted these babies and were very protective of them. One of the babies was named after Michael and the old herdboy, Philemon, who looked after the elephants called him Mikey.

Ironically, no one, ever, had referred to Michael as Mike or Mickey or whatever other abbreviation is suited to the name. I am sure that if they had they would have met with that stony stare that was Michael's trademark. Philemon, however, never received so much as a frown when he referred to 'Baas Michael's baby, Mikey'.

Reluctantly I parked the Landrover and gathered my briefcase with the notes for the service. My poems and little notes from his labourers who wanted to say something but were too shy to stand up and do so. There were also the telegrams that had flooded into the business that his secretary had passed onto me to read out.

As I stood there looking at the sky, which by now was streaming with golden sunlight and making a halo around the Koppies in the distance, a huge black eagle – a Lammergeier – rose from a clump of Acacias and flew overhead. I gazed after him and watched as he flew over the stone chapel, circling lazily. I called to him, speaking softly, saying words of pain and sorrow and thanking him for his presence. He instilled the knowledge that death is not the end – that the soul does fly free.

Walking into the coolness of the Chapel I was struck by the hundreds of flowers placed everywhere, on the pews, the little altar, the floor space was covered. There were elaborate floral arrangements, bouquets, jam jars with proteas and wildflowers, all signatures of the many different types of people involved in Michael's life.

To one side stood a magnificent carving of an eagle. This carving had taken four months to complete and had been done by his 'bossboy', Vuzi, on his game farm. Vuzi had been a street urchin in the alleys of Johannesburg.

Michael had rescued him and taken him to the game farm where he was taught to love the African bush with the same commitment and spiritual awareness as his 'master'. When Vuzi had heard that Michael had become ill and had a limited time to live, he had commenced work on the carving telling Michael that the carving would house his spirit and he would fly forever.

I touched the eagle, running my hands over the magnificent wood, rich yellow and dark patches in places. I did not know the origin and wondered whether it came from a tree on the game farm. I picked it up and noted with surprise that it was not that heavy, despite it's size. It seemed to float in my arms. I carried it to the altar and placed it to the side. Next to it I placed a little calabash made by Michael's maid at the game farm. She had filled it with African violets, his favourite flower.

Looking around me I wondered where all the people coming to say goodbye were going to sit. The Chapel could hold a maximum of 25 people – the rest would have to sit on the grass outside. Gavin, Michael's accountant, had organised a truckload of plastic chairs and a microphone as well as a stereo player so we could play his favourite song.

As I started arranging the flowers and funeral notices I heard the scuffling of what sounded like a dog trying to get through the half closed chapel door. I looked up to see the wrinkled, black face of the resident 'Sangoma' (witchdoctor). She had lived in a cave on this farm for more years than anyone knew.

As the farm had passed from one set of owners to the other, each new set had merely left her to live in peace. Perhaps the superstition of her craft had made them reluctant to evacuate her, who knows. She was truly ancient. No one knew exactly how old she was. There was talk that she was 110 years old but that was always scoffed at by the whites.

She had one badly crippled leg and used a gnarled stick to walk with. She was completely bowed over, her face almost touching her knees.

I stood quietly as she shuffled up the narrow little aisle. I knew that I should not speak first. The respected and wise old Sangoma had to open the conversation and in terms of African ethics I had to defer to her age-old customs.

She leaned her stick on the wooden pew and sank down onto the slasto floor. Resting to catch her breath, she sat with half closed eyes. With wrinkled, twisted old hands she scratched through her many pockets. Her task was made difficult by the faded blanket she wore around her shoulders like a cape. It was tied under her chin with a large safety pin. Eventually she found what she was looking for and in slow movements, taking deep breaths, she tugged and pulled until she got the little bag out of the hidden pocket somewhere in her tribal garment.

Rheumy eyes, crusted and opaque, now stared at me. I could see her blinking to focus better and I waited in awe. I had heard so much about this particular Sangoma. She was a legend in this community. She lived in a cave on the side of one of the bigger hills and only the local chief was allowed to visit her.

A dry, rasping cough made her lean forward. I almost reached out to catch her; afraid she was going to fall on her face. I pulled back and watched her. She stayed like that, nose almost on the floor, still clutching the dirty little bag. I could smell the odours of the bush in her, the open fires made in the cave, the constant boiling and preparing of herbs and other strange ingredients for the Muti that she was so famous for. I knew without looking too hard that the little bag would have been made from the intestine of some animal.

She lifted her head and made strange guttural sounds – grunting noises, wheezing and sniffing, almost as if she was talking to bush animals. I stepped closer, wary at first but realising that she was talking to me. I knelt down and put both my hands flat on the floor. A sign of touching Mother Earth and greeting this Mother of the Tribe.

Then I heard the words, in halting Afrikaans and mingled with Xhosa. They were not making sense and I tried harder to distinguish them. "Die Tokoloshe hy kom, die Wit Tokoloshe hy maak nie mooi nie."

She held out the little bag and I bowed my head in thanks.

More coughing but she was watching intently as I opened the bag. Inside were five little stones, all different in shape and colour. They were smooth and coated in a white powder, which I guessed would have been ground from bones or even dried snake skins. I took them in my hands, feeling their warmth.

She motioned me to open my hand and she took one back.

Translated, this is what she said: "This is you, your life is torn. Much pain and fear. Fear not go away. Too much water from eyes, spilling on sand. Make sick, make tired."

She leaned back, seemingly exhausted, closed her eyes. Struggling for breath. I saw the toothless mouth go slack, fall open. She drew in many little gasps of air, gaining strength to carry on.

She beckoned for the second stone. "This the lion. He rest now. Fly with big bird. He will come back and take you when time is good. He look on you now."

My pain overflowed. I closed my eyes tightly willing myself not to cry. No good, the tears were coursing down my cheeks. I could not suppress the sobs.

The ancient old witchdoctor, still leaning back, fixed those half closed colourless eyes on me and bored into my very soul.

I held my hands open, the three remaining stones waiting for her. Slowly she shook her head, took a long crackling breath and in an absolutely clear voice, suddenly sounding much younger than her body marked her, said, "You must be careful. Your father is talking. Go far away, over the big water – do not come back."

I put the stones back into the funny little bag and held my hands together as if in prayer mode. I closed my eyes and listened to her as she drifted in and out of her mystical chanting.

I got up, leaving her to rest and carried on with arranging the chapel. A minute later she seemed to have fallen into a deep sleep. I left her in peace, her crooked back wedged up against the time-worn wood of the bench.

Cars were pulling up outside and there were murmured conversations. The little chapel would be packed to capacity soon. Then I heard the hearse pull up to the door and the sounds of the trolley being unloaded.

The tall man from the funeral parlour walked in holding his hands clasped in front of him looking as if he was going up for communion. "Morning Mrs Grant, how are we today? I have the dearly departed here." I suddenly saw the humour in his words and the laugh gurgled up from my tummy, breaking the spell of painful hurting.

Michael would be fuming and spitting venomous words at being described in this way. I expected him to cause the coffin to fall off the trolley and waited for that deep-throated laugh of his. It never came and I realised, again, that I was alone. My soul mate could share this funny incident but we could not communicate.

The coffin was decked with an enormous bouquet of Arum

lilies, another of his favourite flowers. The professional mourner and his accomplice had to lift it high off the carved wooden trestle and carry it over the sleeping witchdoctor. They placed it on the floor by the altar and then lifted the trestle over her body.

The coffin and flowers were carefully rearranged. "She'll have to move," the funeral parlour employee said irritably at this hitch in his plans for the dearly departed's sending off.

"No she wont, just leave her where she is. She is here to say goodbye to Michael." I couldn't resist the little test. "Besides, you wouldn't want to annoy a Sangoma would you, she could toor you!"

I had to turn away before I convulsed with laughter at the look of horror on his face. Here was a man who dealt with the dead on a daily basis and he quaked at the thought of the supernatural. Strange isn't it?

An hour later the service had been conducted in accordance with Michael's wishes and it was my duty to close it. I read my farewell poem to a hushed gathering of people. They came from all races and backgrounds. The Chapel was overflowing. People were gathered outside on the grass. Some of them sitting on brightly coloured Sotho blankets, dressed in their ethnic colours as tradition demands. When they came to bid their loved ones farewell they dressed according to the ancient rites of their tribes.

The city dwellers, perspiring in their suits and ties seemed incongruous in these idyllic surroundings. The Sangoma stayed where she was, eyes closed and her breathing barely discernible. The microphone rigged for the occasion had proved to be a necessity.

I kept my hand in my jacket pocket, feeling the warmth of the three little stones and said my farewell:

MICHAEL

Roam free and feel our love go with you.
Eternity has always been there – we live it.
We flow with you, forever knowing
that you made our lives so much richer,
wiser and often times you created a calmness,
when all around us the world
was spinning out of control.
For all the wonderful times we shared with you.
Your face when doing what you loved best,
flying way above clouds and floating downward
You saw pictures and stories in the clouds.
Now, you are going to live them.
*Stay close, but don't make **our** problems yours!*

Michael, my friend, this is from me.
Thank you, from the bottom of my heart
For all the wisdom, the love, the support,
The sounds of many silences,
The sunsets and early dawns on African plains.
All the stories you told me.

The way you touched my life,
The deepest understanding I have known.
I will miss you forever – ask you to fly with me
on my journeys,
Help me to make good decisions.
You said your spirit would not leave forever –
Just take short journeys with loved ones.
I stand in line for you to touch me.
I weep for the loss of you.
I love you, we love you – forever.

After the commemoration service the caterers started moving amongst the crowd offering drinks and snacks. I expected the mood to lift but it didn't. The stillness of the air seemed to make everyone more lethargic and conversation was muted. The African women assembled in the main car park and started their traditional dances of farewell. Their ululating echoed against the nearby koppies and seemed to have a distinct refrain coming from that direction.

Linda, with John Slabbert in tow, stood way back under the shade of a Jacaranda. Glass in one hand, cigarette in the other. I deliberately avoided her glance. She would undoubtedly have had something cattish to say about my farewell speech. She had not contacted me since the lunch date and, to my surprise, was ignoring her old staff. About fifteen of the mourners were Michael's staff from his home and the game farm. Some of them, if not all of them, had at one stage worked for Linda during the course of their marriage.

I knew most of the staff and walked into the warmth of their African emotion. Raw sorrow lined their faces but the total acceptance of Michael's death was taken in ethnic spirit. He was now free to roam on the plains with his forefathers and grow wiser with their guidance. He would, in turn, become a spirit teacher and so the wisdom would be passed on into eternity. Vusi, who lived on the game farm, came up to me with a small bunch of roses.

"Madam Verryn, these are for you. The Boss planted this bush for you. He gave it your name."

I looked into those darkest of black eyes, the face etched with grief. The shared feelings of loss was too much for me to handle. I swallowed hard, found no words but took the little posy and clutched it to my chest.

I made my way to my car and drove up the sand road as far as the base of the nearest koppie. I stood staring into the sky trying to make out a story. I wanted a picture story to console me. I did not want to see that long black hearse drive away to a destination where Michael would be cremated. He would be gone. Forever.

CHAPTER TWENTY- SIX

Degradation

It was three weeks since the arrest. I had spent countless hours in consultation with lawyers and advocates.

My legal team was more interested in the divorce action than the criminal matter. The divorce trial would earn them mega bucks and they did not really know how to handle the other issue. They were adamant that this had been a grave miscarriage of justice but were reluctant to commit themselves to taking on the State for wrongful arrest. With so many black lawyers and advocates now entering the legal profession it was definitely a case of 'keeping your nose clean'. You never knew who may or may not be a beneficial contact in the long run. Obviously, behind closed doors, they slated the system and made hugely derogatory comments, but ask them to do something about it? It was procrastination in a big way. They kept urging me to wait until Sonja, the investigating officer, came up with her so-called evidence.

My lawyer kept telling me that Trevor had bribed someone. There were no real charges. The file was empty and the list of excuses was endless. In addition, he had no respect for his partner who handled the 'criminal' side of the business. He openly slated this partner of his and I lost total confidence in their ability to protect me.

My legal fees were mounting by the minute and I roughly made a calculation. A staggering total of R425,000 ($106,250) to date and I was nowhere near winning a divorce, or more importantly, clearing my name of the vexatious charges laid by my spouse. I kept thinking that the New South Africa portrayed internationally was in total contrast to what was happening in the country.

My most important goal was to get my passport back and return to Australia and try to recover some strength and concentrate on business issues. I wanted to take my mind off the horror of the past weeks and allow myself to grieve for Michael.

My lawyer, at my insistence, appointed a senior advocate to handle the criminal matter. This man, Nolan Amory, was well into his seventies and had already retired. He was reputed to have been one of the best in the country. He was bad news for me. He constantly lost important documents, misunderstood briefings and produced nonsensical affidavits. Every meeting I had with him ended with me in tears. Tears of frustration and fear of not getting the matter resolved. In the end I resorted to doing his filing for him to ensure sure the safety of important papers.

We were working to a strong deadline and he had to produce a convincing affidavit that would result in me getting back my passport and being given permission to leave the country. It was completely wrong. If we had used this document I am sure we would have never have got my passport back. It would have been confiscated and I would have borne the brunt of Trevor's anger. After weeks of preparation we rejected this ridiculous document and started over.

At last we were given a court date for the application. I was exhausted. The preceding weeks had been one long legal meeting. I had hardly spent time with Kelly. She was writing exams and studying. I felt guilty that I could not cook her those special little meals we used to put so much emphasis on. They used to be for building stamina and loaded with the right vitamins.

In the meantime, twice a week, Mondays and Friday, I was subject to the ultimate humiliation and degradation. Undoubtedly, this had been one of Trevor's stipulations. He would have known how every incident would have eroded my self-confidence. Every incident would have been a lesson in humility. He was wrong in the end because my strength of character carried me through this period and I came through it smiling.

On these days, between the hours of 6 a.m. and 6 p.m., I had to call in at the local police station and sign in. This was to ensure that I was not hiding an Ozzie passport somewhere and had not left the country. I should have been that lucky!

Signing in was a comedy of errors. There was a bright green Lever Arch file kept underneath the counter in the charge office. Marked in heavy black strokes it read 'PAROLE'. There were loose forms inside for all those who had had their wings clipped and had to suffer the smirking attention of the keepers of the law.

The first morning I had to sign in, the Monday after the arrest, I forced myself to walk into that police station holding my head high and a smile on my face. Inside, I was quivering with trepidation, my tummy felt like it was full of agitated butterflies.

Behind the desk were two female constables – white South Africans. This immediately struck me as unusual. This particular police station had a strong contingent of black policemen and in the past they had been most kind and efficient when we had needed their help.

The two women were having a private discussion. "Can we help you?" The young blonde woman was friendly.

"Yes, I have come to sign."

"Sign? What do you have to sign?"

My throat constricted. I stood there staring, the words

would not come out. "I was arrested last week and all I know is I have to sign a book here every Monday and Friday." My voice broke and I felt the sting of the tears.

They instantly gave me their undivided attention. "You what?" The brunette had been casually taking in my jewellery and clothing.

"My husband has framed me – please let me sign and get out of here." I was dreading anyone else coming into the office and adding to my embarrassment. However, the two quizzy ladies would not let me go. They asked a string of questions and satisfied their curiosity. At no stage were they supercilious – they genuinely could not believe the tale they were hearing.

"My God, what is this country coming to? We are battling to arrest a woman who defrauded her employers of millions of Rands and they arrest you on suspicion and hearsay!"

The blonde had located the file, which I got to know so well – the 'Parole' file. When she opened it there were no documents with my name on them.

"Are you sure that you really were arrested and taken to *proper* court?" My sense of humour rose to the surface, lessening the humiliation and confusion I was feeling.

"Seeing as I don't have experience of too many courts, I really don't know what a 'proper' court is, but I think the one they took me to was real. There were many heartbroken and worried people milling around and, of course, there were Prosecutors, decked out in their austere robes. Then, there was also a very important man sitting on a platform, I think they called him 'your Honour'."

The two women started laughing and the threatened tears dried.

"Well, we don't have anything on you, so you can come back on Friday. Nowadays they take forever to get paper work through. It's the system you know. The New South Africa and all that." The brunette spoke with a marked accent. You could see she hated her job.

"No, I will not go away unless I have signed some form of documentation. I am not giving my husband the slightest opportunity to harass me any further."

"Ja, you could be right. We'll just let you sign in the Incident Book." The blonde hauled the massive book forward and I wrote my name, the time and signed next to it.

When I walked out of there the unreality of my situation hit me with such force. I could hardly breathe and I struggled to unlock my car door. Suddenly, with absolute clarity, I realised that I was not *free*.

At this stage I had not even read any of the terms and conditions of my 'bail'. My lawyer had taken all the documentation with him. Later that day I found out that I was not allowed to leave Gauteng, the province in which I lived. I could not go away for a few days of holiday. I could not live a normal life as a South African citizen. I was not allowed to go anywhere near an international airport. I was a detainee whether I liked it or not. Boy, were they making sure I did not skip the country! They also ensured that I was restricted to Bedfordview and this meant that Trevor could harass me to his heart's content. And he did.

Later on, after 'signing in' six times or so, I had got to know most of the cops who worked at the station. I used to go very early, as soon after 6 a.m. as I could, so that I would not bump into anyone I knew. The village is small and its inhabitants suffered a never-ending spate of hijacking, stolen cars, muggings and housebreakings. People were forever trekking to the cops to open files.

The majority of the uniformed cops were friendly and seemed to have empathy for my situation. They laughed and joked with me once the initial surprise had worn off. Most of them knew me by name and I used to get the "Hi Verryn, how are you," more often than not. Slowly I started feeling less embarrassed and more furious at the injustice of it all. Then one morning I was subjected to the venom of reverse racialism.

It was a Friday and the office was deserted that time of the morning. I was feeling good, I was going to have a game of golf with David as soon as I finished my clocking in.

"Yes, what can I do for you?" I had not seen this sergeant before.

Pointing to the green file, "I've come to sign the Parole file."

He looked me up and down, his dark brown eyes travelling from the tips of my shoes to my head.

"You on parole? What did you do?" The black skin of his forearms made a stark contrast to the green as he folded his arms and rested them on the file.

Once again I had to blurt out the story, by now becoming like a constant refrain.

"For how much?" His lips parted in a thin smile, snow-white teeth showing.

"Excuse me, what do you mean – how much?"

Irritable now, "How much money, how much did you defraud?"

My blood started boiling. I did not have to be interrogated by a cop. I had already been subjected to the worst kind of degradation – now this on top of it.

"I'm not sure and I do not want to discuss it here. Can I have the file please?"

"Who is your husband?" He ignored my request and held onto the file.

"Trevor Grant."

"Eh, Trevor Grant from up the road? Ha ha, we know him. He is the gangster, maybe he should be signing and not you!"

The phone on the desk started ringing and he handed me

the file. I signed and almost flew out of there.

After that incident I vowed not to let these excursions to the police station upset me. I adopted a stronger and more confident manner and started going in at different times, whether the place was packed or not. Many a quizzical stare was thrown my way by the righteous civilians reporting the crimes against them. I used to look at them, men and women and think to myself, "How little you know. How fragile your existence is. Anyone in South Africa can go to the police; lay charges against you and you will be arrested. You will then be at the mercy of the system and like me, you will bear the scars on your soul forever."

CHAPTER TWENTY-SEVEN

Freedom again

The day of the court application for the release of the bail conditions rolled around. Eventually, after many hours of legal consultation, rewriting affidavits and putting up with Nolan's irritating behaviour, we stood outside the Prosecutor's office.

She kept us waiting for 15 minutes and beckoned us in with no greeting. Her office was as bleak as her personality and she obviously hated her job as well. I had not yet come across a person within the legal system who seemed to enjoy their days at work.

Nolan spoke first. "We are going to request that Mrs Grant's passport be returned and would like to know how far you have got with your investigations."

Her reaction was exactly the opposite of what I was expecting. I had been briefed by the lawyers and had been dreading this meeting. Prosecutors wielded tremendous power.

"We will grant the request but she will have to pay higher bail."

"Very well, that takes care of that, but what about the charges? Where is the charge sheet?" Nolan was aggressive. He leaned forward and grabbed the yellow folder with my name printed on it and flipped it open. He frightened me with his tone, as I wanted to humour this young woman who held my future in her hands.

"Where is the documentation for the so-called charges? What evidence of fraud is there?"

She snatched the file. Her face closed off and she spoke in clipped tones "Listen here, Mr Amory, we are doing you a favour. Don't ask questions outside of the courtroom. We are investigating and that's it!" He scrutinised her, the pause was deafening in it's intensity. I would have kicked him under the desk if she would not have seen it.

His question was loaded. "Are you going to speak to the Magistrate before court or should I do so. I would like him to know that you have agreed to this before we go in front of the bench."

"Not necessary, we have put the papers forward, he knows about it. She has to pay in a further R45,000 ($11,250) and she will get her passport back." A spur of the moment financial calculation and that signalled the end of the meeting.

We walked into the corridor, not saying goodbye to her, she had turned her back on us. We made our way through the maze of passages and doorways. The filth and litter in this building was too much to comprehend. Surely the administration of the legal platforms could uphold cleanliness and order.

Nolan walked with his head bowed and kicked a coke can out of his way.

"Just look at this filth, can you believe that these corridors of justice used to be immaculate and well maintained. Look at the filthy walls, look at the graffiti. This is fucking chaos. This country is going to the dogs," he muttered incessantly.

As we drew closer to the courtroom, ironically number 13, my heart started pounding and memories of the arrest flooded back. I stopped in mid stride and Nolan carried on. He became aware that I was not with him and turned around. I stood looking at my feet, gasping for air. This was a major panic attack.

Grabbing my arm, he pulled me forward. "Come on, this is

the last leg. Let's get this over and done with so you can head for Australia. That officious bitch is shit scared. They know they have overstepped the mark this time and they are going to cover their arses, you mark my words."

The courtroom was packed. I could not bring myself to look around. I sat on the same spot as before, staring at my nails. Nolan disappeared to find the Magistrate. He had decided to ignore the Prosecutor's instructions.

My name was called first. I went into the box and it was over within two minutes.

Sonja was standing outside and as she handed me my passport I looked deep into her eyes. She could not hold my gaze and looked away.

"God Bless you, Mrs Grant, have a good trip to Australia."

I said nothing, just stared at her and slowly put my passport in my bag.

She felt my disdain and I sensed her uncertainty. "Just make sure you return in two months for the next court appearance. You have to be here or else..."

I smiled, inwardly gathering strength. "By then, will you have the evidence you are seeking and will your investigations be complete?' My tone carried the sarcasm to its hilt.

Nolan laughed out loud as she walked away.

I made that old man run to my car, which was parked a block away from the court building. I was free and my joyousness in this little triumph over Trevor's evil made me want to run as fast as my legs would carry me. I walked so fast he was wheezing when we pulled out into the busy traffic.

I dropped him off at his offices and headed for home. I had a tentative golf date with Kate and had to phone my brothers with the good news. I could now go and book my ticket back to Oz and catch the next flight out in three day's time.

CHAPTER TWENTY-EIGHT

The currency smuggler

Kate and I were on our way to play golf. My nightmare ordeal was over and I could now act 'normal'.

As we drove to the security company to pick up our guard for the afternoon, I gave her the rundown on that morning's events at court. She was in stitches listening to me recount old Nolan's mutterings and foul language. Neither of us had ever expected an advocate to swear so much!

The security guard, Johnson, who I always booked to accompany me on my golf days, was a tall, heavily built Zulu of about 40. He wore the regulation uniform of his company, navy and white and he also wore a visible bullet-proof vest. His huge pistol was tucked into the flap of the vest. He wore heavy army type boots and his attitude was courteous but serious. A quiet man, he had, over the last year or so, whilst guarding me on the golf course, learned so much about the game that he often told me what club to use. He had, prior to working for me, never been on a golf course in his life.

When I tell my friends in Australia that I had to have an armed guard with me on the golf course, they think I am joking. It was no joke. A main road divided our golf course with nine holes on either side of it. The club management would not follow the example set by most other golf clubs by putting electric fencing around the entire property with guards at the entrance gates. The club felt that it would be too expensive an exercise and left it open. Over the previous year, in quick succession, there had already been six muggings and a rape.

The muggers would hide in the bushes at certain secluded holes. They would time their attacks and would hold guns or knives to the player's throats and rob them of their clubs, wallets, cell phones and jewellery. On one occasion, they even made one of the players strip down to his underwear, as they liked his clothing and his golf shoes. The rape incident was tragic and this happened early one Saturday morning when a guy and his girlfriend were accosted. He had been made to watch as four tsotsis raped her.

After this incident I decided to hire a guard every time I played there. On my first game, with Johnson in tow, the caddies all went on strike as they thought he was going to take business away from them. I had to hire a caddy to pull my golf cart and Johnson walked along with darting eyes searching for strange vehicles parked along the skirting roadway or for loiterers skulking in the bushes. He was a very intimidating person and the caddies treated him with utmost respect. Needless to say, all the ladies in the club used to make a dash for the player's program. They all wanted to play with me, as they would be protected! Before this there were many who considered themselves too good to play with me.

As we pulled into the gates of the golf club I felt a strange emptiness welling up inside of me. This would probably be the last time I played golf in South Africa. I was leaving soon and I knew I had to come back for the court actions but that would be for a couple of weeks at a time. I was soon to leave my roots and I had to make the strongest effort to settle down in my new country. This feeling, combined with the constant dull ache of the loss of Michael, made me slip into one of my all too common quiet moods. Suddenly, I did not feel like playing.

"Come on Verryn, don't look so down. You've just been telling me about your legal victory!" Kate swung down from the Land Rover and started helping Johnson unload the golf trolleys.

I resolved to play well and be good company for my darling friend.

We were on the 11th hole and I had just teed off with my Biggest Big Bertha. The ball travelled for roughly one hundred and eighty metres straight down the fairway and I was feeling good. I heard the ringing of the cell phone and knew that Johnson would answer for me. He had become so accomplished I used to be teased that he was my golf day secretary.

"Madam, this man says it is urgent." He handed me the phone.

Stepping aside so as not worry Kate with her first shot I took the phone.

"Verryn Grant speaking."

"Mrs Grant, my name is Mr Ashton. I am a senior investigator for the South African Reserve Bank."

I almost dropped the phone, my legs wanted to give way.

"We would like to come and see you immediately with regard to currency smuggling."

"Currency smuggling, what do you mean? Is this another one of my husband's vile deeds?"

"Unfortunately, we cannot disclose who reported you. When can we see you?"

"I will have to speak to my attorneys and you can see me at their offices. Will that be okay?"

I was learning how to deal with intimidation. Trevor's campaign of terror had already taught me many things. Despite my coolness of tone I was fragmented inside. I could feel my heart pumping inside of my mouth and I knew I had to cut the conversation short before I collapsed on the grass. I told Kate.

"The bastard, when is he going to get his due? He is the one that smuggles money. Everybody in Bedfordview knows about his cartel. I cannot believe this!" She threw her club on the ground and folded me in her arms.

Between her and Johnson they managed to get me back to the vehicle as I stumbled along on legs that had turned to jelly.

When I got home I phoned Leon and told him about the call. He said he would phone Ashton and set up an appointment for the next day. I had better postpone my trip to Australia.

The following day I rose early, phoned the funeral directors and asked the friendly administrative clerk when Michael's ashes would be available. I had to arrange for them to be scattered at the game farm as Linda wanted to be there. She had phoned me the previous evening and told me she wanted to get back to Portugal in a hurry. I had, in any event, planned this final farewell for the last day before I left for Australia.

The ashes were ready, I could collect them. She wished me a happy day.

I phoned Leon, he had arranged the meeting with Ashton for 2 p.m.

Taking half of one of the little pink tranquillisers I had been given weeks ago, I ate an apple and drank two cups of coffee. Kelly was in her study, she was still writing exams and I had not told her about the latest development.

"Bye, Kells, I'm going to pick up Michael's ashes and then going to see Linda to make arrangements. See you later this afternoon."

"Mom, before you go, tell me what's wrong?"

"What do you mean, my darling... nothing's wrong." I gave her my widest smile.

"Mom, please don't hide things from me. I *know* you're fretting about something, your light was on the whole night last night."

Putting my arms around her, this tall, beautiful girl with cascading honey-coloured hair, hugged me back with such strength and love. I could feel her heartbeat and I closed my eyes in silent prayer for her being.

"I'm okay, Kells, see you this afternoon." I kissed her and rushed for the door.

Braamfontein was very crowded that morning. I drove around looking for parking in the car park belonging to the funeral parlour. It was full, there were funeral services going on in both the side chapels. Wishing that I was not in the BMW but in the Landy when I could have parked on the pavement, I drove into the street and found a spot about 200 metres away. I fastened the top button of my blouse so that a would-be mugger would not see the embossed gold chain I was wearing. I took my two diamond rings off and surreptitiously shoved them under the mat by my feet. I took my watch off and slid it into my jacket pocket. Now I was ready to unlock my car doors and all I had to do was sprint to the building, making sure that I was not being followed and praying that my car would not be stolen or broken into.

Out of breath but safe, clutching my handbag under my arm, the strap wrapped around my wrist, I asked the receptionist for the ashes. I was made to sign a logbook and was given a carved wooden casket with a little silver plaque on it. 'Michael Brent 1946-1998'. It felt so light. I had subconsciously expected Michael's ashes to have the weight of his tremendous personal dynamism. Strange how one's mind thinks sometimes.

This time I walked slowly back to the car. Somehow I felt protected. Once more, I had Michael close to me. I was holding the casket in front of me staring at the intricate carving – my bag swinging casually from my left shoulder.

I almost walked into the man blocking my path. He was young, barely 18, his face bore a vivid scar from below the left eyebrow right down to the chin. An obvious stab wound. His eyes were like slits. I stopped, staring straight at those slanting eyes. His face was very pointed. Most unusual for the ethnic features in South Africa. He looked at the casket – I looked at the casket.

Just then I became aware of the second man and I knew without doubt that I was going to be robbed. The second one, older and taller, was right at my side, brushing against my shoulder. He had come from the rear. My car was less than 10 metres away.

"Give me your bag and your keys." He slid his shirt sleeve up and I saw the long blade held in his hand, the handle well concealed by his arm under the sleeve. He was so close to me now, I smelt his sour breath.

What I did next I will never know why. "Hold this, I'll give you my keys." I held the casket out for him so that I could get the keys in my pocket.

With a look of horror on his face, he stepped back, "Aikona – that is the dead!"

The other man bumped my shoulder and made as if to grab my bag but he got momentarily distracted by his partner yelling. I took the gap and shouted, "The dead will get you, you swine!"

With the sound of rubber soles hitting the uneven pavement at a heck of a rate, I watched the two products of the Apartheid years run off into the crowded streets. I had experienced another commonplace incident in South Africa and I was lucky that I had come off lightly. Michael had, once again, saved the day!

I got into my car, surprised that I was so calm. How could I be afraid to face Mr Ashton after this?

Later that afternoon, having had the meeting with the lawyers and representatives of the Reserve Bank I was fully in the picture. Trevor had reported me to the Reserve Bank as a currency smuggler big time! He had told them that I owned a business in Australia and that I smuggled money on every trip out of the country.

Not all, but many South Africans now living in Australia are currency smugglers if you want to use Trevor's claim to the title. Currently, one is allowed to take R100,000 ($25,000) per annum out of the country. This is for business or holiday use. We would bring out the maximum amount allowed and then deposit it into our bank accounts every trip we made to Australia. However, the bulk of our money, my two daughters' and mine, came out of an international bank account in Europe. When Rowan died, many years ago, he had left both the girls and myself a sizeable inheritance in a trust fund with this bank. My daughters were only allowed access to their inheritances when they turned 25. I had left my money in the fund, as I knew it would be more beneficial offshore than bringing it to South Africa.

When we bought the business in Brisbane we paid for it out of monies transferred from Europe. Trevor knew about these transactions. He had told the Reserve Bank everything about us but not about himself.

For many years Trevor had been smuggling money out of the country. He used many avenues: travel agents who specialised in laundering money, diamond smugglers who flew them out via Zimbabwe in private planes. He paid wages to the wives of men who worked overseas and these men then deposited dollars into his Swiss bank accounts. He was a master at currency smuggling.

How he had the audacity to report me and not run the risk of me spilling the beans on him, I will never know. All I can think of is that he was so intent on nailing me to the wall that he became irrational and did not think about the serious consequences of his hate campaign.

I told the Reserve Bank officials everything I knew and suddenly the emphasis swung from Mrs Grant to Mr Grant. I was told that I could still leave the country; they had no charges or investigation pending. They were happy with the meeting and they were now intent on going after the 'Big Fish'. I gave them my home and work telephone numbers in Australia and walked out of that meeting thanking God for yet another escape from the clutches of the devil himself.

This incident was only one of many of Trevor wreaking havoc in my life. His campaign of terror and victimisation carried on for two years bringing me to my knees and causing utter destruction in my life and those of my two daughters. My legal fees were well over one million rand ($250,000) and the winners of the game have only been the lawyers.

CHAPTER TWENTY-NINE

Michael's ashes go home

Kelly and I had set off early. The trip to Phalaborwa would take us five hours in the Land Rover. I had sold my BMW the day before. She had been named Emmaleen. She was only two years old and immaculate with only 30,000 on the clock. The motor dealer drove off with a smile from ear to ear. She was an excellent buy. I was sad to see her go.

Never mind, the Landy was just as luxurious, just not as fast. Kelly sat back with eyes closed, humming to the music. As I drove, my mind wandered over the past few years. Michael was very prominent in my thoughts. The little casket with the remains of this powerful, kind, unusual man, was carefully propped up on the back seat, a bunch of Proteas protecting it.

Linda was meeting us at Falcon's Rest. How she was getting there I did not know. She declined when I asked her if she wanted a lift. I hoped with all my heart that she was not going to bring Slabbert with her. Although I did not know him he did not strike me as having been a friend of Michael's.

I had spoken to Vusi on the phone and he was preparing a feast for us. He would also take us to the lookout, deep in the bush, where we were going to scatter Michael's ashes.

Kelly was looking forward to this overnight stay at the game farm, as she had not been there for a couple of years.

We were tired and thirsty and took the turnoff onto the dirt road. A kilometre down the road we pulled up at the hut serving as the access control centre. The guards on duty spent their days sheltering from the hot sun and their nights safe from wild animals. We greeted the smiling man in his khaki uniform and he lifted the boom across the entrance. We had another 50 odd kilometres to go and we were in game country. About five game farm owners owned the stretch of road collectively. They had pooled their funds and built this access road.

It was common to sight a herd of elephant on this stretch of road. They usually kept away from the road and had become accustomed to the four-wheel drive vehicles travelling up and down. The drivers were mostly game wardens working on the game farms and employees of the environmental protection organisations. Guests visiting the game farms seldom drove their own vehicles along the rutted roads. They normally flew into the airport in the town and were picked up by the wardens in open Land Rovers. This was the start of their safari.

I drove slowly, enjoying the smell of the bush. The unique aroma of grass, sand and dense bush combined with the anticipation of seeing at least a few of the Big Five en route to the homestead made me heady with love for my land. I did not know when the next time would be. I was emigrating to a country that had different kinds of wild animals.

We encountered a herd of Cape buffalo and a lonely hyena before stopping at the entrance to the homestead. Vusi met us smiling from ear to ear, immaculate in his khaki uniform with highly polished boots and belt. He pressed the remote to open the heavy metal gates.

"Sabona, Madam, you are welcome!"

The striking white teeth gleamed in the sunlight, the smile like blazing sunlight.

"Vusi, it is good to see you. How is Angel?" Angel was his little daughter, she had been very ill. Michael had called in the local doctor who had diagnosed her as suffering from a form of meningitis. Vusi had also taken her to a neighbouring Sangoma for a second opinion. Michael had gladly paid for the mixture of herbs and medicines but had extracted a promise that she would also be fed the course of antibiotics prescribed by the doctor.

"Angel is getting better. She wants to go back to school now."

Elsie, the homestead cook, walked across the wooden verandah wiping her hands on her apron, she was short, round and cuddly and carrying too much weight, good testimony to her skills. We hugged and I could see the tears glistening on the shiny black cheeks.

"Hau, Kelly, you are so big! You not little girl anymore." She embraced Kelly and as I watched my daughter bend down in greeting to this African matron, I had a vivid flashback of Lizzie, the maid who had nursed all three of my girls. Lizzie had worked for us for 25 years before she retired to her own tribal village deep in the Drakensberg Mountains.

Without saying anything I took the little casket from the back seat and handed it to Vusi. He did not make eye contact and walked away holding it as I had seen him holding a baby bird that had fallen out of it's nest a long time ago. I carried the proteas and handed them to Sanna, the shy young maid hovering at the door.

Our luggage was taken into the house while we gratefully helped ourselves to a drink on the verandah. Sinking into the leather and wood chairs we sat back listening to the loud and excited chatter as Elsie issued a stream of instructions to the junior maids in the kitchen

Vusi had taken my keys and driven the Land Rover around the back to the garage area where it would be washed and cleaned by the yard staff.

Kelly and I went off to our rooms to shower. Linda was expected within the hour, according to Vusi.

Kelly and I were back on the veranda feeling refreshed with

cold Coronas in hand and starting to get really hungry. The setting sun had turned the sky into hues of red and gold. It was accentuated by the darkness rolling over the bush land, the stark shapes of trees and koppies were outlined in a silvery glow, a reflection of the greens and yellows everywhere. That time of the year, the beginning of the dry season, the veld takes on a palette of it's own.

The throaty roar of the powerful engine broke my reverie. I saw the metallic red of the 4 x 4 and was struck by the contrasting background as it came to a halt just below us. My heart sank, Slabbert was driving. He was going to be present at this final farewell to Michael after all.

"Howzit Verryn. You look gorgeous." He stepped onto the veranda, ignoring Vusi's outstretched hand for the keys. He swaggered up to us with Linda following closely. As he bent forward in an attempt to kiss me hello I moved away and his mouth brushed my cheek. He reeked of alcohol and I watched in disgust as he tried the same tactic on Kelly. She too moved out of his way and he did not get to make contact. He had never met Kelly, he hardly knew me and here he was, acting like a long lost friend.

I knew instinctively that Michael could not have liked this man. He was too smooth, too insincere. Michael kept his distance from men like this. He had many business associates but very few friends.

Linda was teetering on her high-heeled sandals. She was wearing white ski pants with a pale pink knitted top. Her jewellery flashed in the dusky light. I looked at the pair of them and thought they suited one another very well. This did not detract from my feeling of absolute disappointment and trepidation. The next 24 hours were going to be stressful.

When the latecomers had showered and changed we sat down to Vusi's feast. He served it on the wide verandah. The long wooden table was set with grass place mats made by the tribal women in the area. The carved candlesticks made of soapstone depicted the animals. Zulu women in the Natal Midlands made the wine glasses. Michael and I had each bought a set of the brightly painted goblets when we had flown to Durban months before. I had forgotten about my set. It was now in a container on a ship destined for Australia.

As Elsie and her juniors served the delicious roast venison with fresh vegetables and a gravy that I have never tasted anywhere else, I watched Linda and her newfound friend. They were obviously well into an affair and the intimacy of their conversation was out of place in front of Kelly.

"What's going to happen with this game farm?" The slack mouth was forced into a smile. I ignored the question, pretending that he was asking Linda.

"Verryn, you know more about Michael's affairs, answer John's question."

"I'm not au fait with Michael's affairs. Gavin is handling everything. I think this farm is going to the Endangered Wild Life Trust." I felt extremely uncomfortable and hoped that would be the end of the conversation.

"What a waste, they wont know what to do with it. Why wasn't it left to Linda?" The intentions became very clear.

"I don't know what is being left to whom. I would appreciate it if you would stop asking personal questions about Michael's affairs." I meant to sound aggressive. This man riled me.

The conversation drifted in and out of current affairs in South Africa and I gleaned the information that Slabbert had sold his business a while ago and was on the look out for some other worthwhile opportunities, like a wealthy lady perhaps? Unfortunately for him Linda had a husband waiting for her in Portugal. No doubt he too was wondering how much she stood to inherit.

I knew that I had to make my excuses and retire to bed before I ended up being rude to someone and regretting it. After all, we had a ceremony to conduct in the morning.

Kelly excused herself and I wandered into the study looking for a book to lull me into sleep.

The study had been Michael's favourite room. He spent many hours alone reading his books and working on his computer. From this room he conducted all his business dealings regarding the many Wild Life Trusts and Environmental Protection Organisations he belonged to. He supported many funds in North Africa and had also become involved in international projects. His passion for animals and the environment was tangible. His love for Africa, the land and its people was evident in the hundreds of books lovingly sorted and stacked on heavy wooden shelves. The solid mahogany desk shone with the love and care bestowed on it by the loyal servants in this house. This was where their beloved Master had found his peace from the hectic city life.

The deep colours of the Persian shiraz covering the floor made stark contrast to the roughly plastered walls. The people living on this farm had built the house and Michael had given them free rein to imprint their talents on his home.

The aura of Michael lingered in this room. I sank down into the leather armchair placed next to the unlit fireplace. It was not cold enough for log fires. In a way I was glad. Memories of cold winter nights in front of this fireplace made me over protective of this room. If there had been a fire, Linda and her companion would undoubtedly have disturbed the calm and serenity of this haven.

I chose a book, *A Day in the Life of an African Elephant*, and went to my room.

CHAPTER THIRTY

Goodbye Michael

At five the next morning I was woken by Sanna. A steaming cup of coffee placed on the bedside table was the signal that I had to get up and prepare for the excursion into the bush. I could hear the diesel engine of the open Land Rover as it was driven to the front of the house. This vehicle had been specially made for game viewing and had wrap-around bullbars for the ultimate in bundu bashing.

We positioned ourselves for the drive. Kelly sat in the passenger seat next to Vusi, John and Linda took up the seat behind the driver and I climbed up to the backseat which was elevated above the other seats. Philemon, broadly smiling and with shotgun in hand, climbed onto the 'tracker' seat. It was 5.30 a.m. and the ground had a light dusting of frost making the grass sparkle and the huge spider webs translucent in the dawn light.

Vusi had already loaded the cooler boxes with breakfast and drinks for the trip. The wooden casket was placed on the front seat between him and Kelly. I remember thinking that he more than likely took it to bed with him the night before. He had no fear of the dead spirit of his Master. His Master was going to stay with him forever. He had told me that on the day of the funeral ceremony.

Linda and her companion were nursing hangovers and their conversation was subdued. Slabbert kept his distance from me and I resolved to carry out Michael's wishes to the letter. He would be put to rest in peace and harmony even if it meant that I used my talent of selective hearing.

We drove through dense bush and the rutted roads led us into many different landscapes. I was always enthralled by the stark contrasts of this land. You could drive through a forested area into a barren stretch of veld dotted with khakibos and then come up to a riverbank, lush with green shrub and willow trees.

Vusi was an expert tracker and he and Philemon pointed out the looming shapes of the elephant herd long before any of the city dwellers saw them. We stopped in awe as the huge animals leisurely crossed the road a hundred metres away from us. Vusi cut the engine and we sat, quietly waiting for them to reach their morning destination in search of the succulent trees in the dense bush dropping away to our left.

We counted 11 with two babies among them. The maternal instinct of the elephant cow is incredibly strong and the trackers knew that you never separated them by driving through the midst of a herd. Young bulls are very protective of their matriarchs and babies. They used to scare tourists with their mock charges. Although we knew all about mock charges we never took them for granted. The animals in the wild are as unpredictable as the human animals in civilisation. There is no behaviour pattern cast in stone. We waited for them to disappear into the glade of trees and Vusi started the engine.

With Philemon keeping track of the footprints in the sand we followed the trail of an old lion. A loner, he was known to the game wardens. He was battle scarred and had seemingly been kicked out of the pride by younger and stronger lions. He was often sighted at the waterhole where we were heading. He hunted the smaller buck drinking at the hole. It was an easier task than taking a zebra on the run. We lost his trail when he veered off into the scrub.

The waterhole was full. The last rains of the summer season

had been good and the surrounding plateau was awash with healthy shrub and vines. Trees half submerged in the water lifted their umbrella-like shapes to the early morning sun for warmth. As we drove up slowly a large black eagle lifted his wings and flew out from his perch high in an acacia tree. He circled lazily, dipping his wings in salute to the Aviator on board. I sent him my silent message of thanks. Every time I see an eagle, in whatever country I find myself, I will know that Michael is close and will listen for the message brought to me.

Vusi parked the vehicle and we stretched our legs. We climbed up the wooden steps to the lookout platform built high in the trees. It had been designed by Michael and was completely disguised by the bush surrounding it. It was semi-circular with stone walls offering protection on three sides. The front was completely open except for a strong wooden balustrade. The base of this platform was reinforced with aluminium struts also disguised within the native bush. Here, you could sit for hours and watch many species of animals in the Kruger Park come down to drink and sometimes bathe and frolic in the clear water. This was one of the few natural spring dams that did not dry out in the winter months and become gaping mud holes churned up by thirsty animals.

Our breakfast was cooked on the gas burners built into a section of the back wall. The slatted table was set with gleaming cutlery and a gaily-coloured tablecloth. The smell of bacon drifting into the air made us realise how hungry we were. The little wooden casket was a heartrending reminder of the man who had made this farm his hideaway and in doing so had not only made a huge contribution to the wellbeing of the many families living on this piece of land but also to the conservation of the animal life. I hope and prayed that people with the same commitment would continue his work.

Breakfast was over and the cooler boxes packed and loaded.

The last act of farewell was looming and we were all very subdued. Linda had been smoking ever since we got into the lookout and I had seen the look of irritation cross Vusi's face. Michael used to smoke but never in the bush. I sensed her feelings of despair and felt like hugging her but could not bring myself to do it. Slabbert was a definite wedge between us.

"Linda, do you want to scatter Michael's ashes?" I picked up the little casket.

"No, you do it, you're good with words. I have not prepared anything."

"Linda, we don't have to say anything, just say Goodbye." Kelly was sensing my unease and came up behind me, putting her arms around me.

"Come on Mom, let's go down to the water and scatter the ashes on the banks."

Vusi and Philemon stood to attention, watching this play of emotions.

Slabbert stood with his hands in his pockets staring out to the hills in the distance.

Linda and I were locked in our misery, unable to make the first move. Our emotions were tangled and similar.

Gently taking the casket out of my hands, Kelly stepped down to the ground and looked up at me with that thick mane of golden hair framing her beautiful face. Her big brown eyes were saying, "You can do it Mom, you must do it."

I stepped down, my legs felt suddenly weak. Vusi was close behind me; he could feel my weakness.

He walked up to Kelly and silently opened the casket. Taking two handfuls of the ashes he turned to me holding out his offering.

I opened my hands and with a shock felt the rough gritty feeling of the remains of Michael. I was blinded by tears and not caring who saw me in this state. Somehow I had expected the ashes to be soft and feathery, that they would blow away in the breeze. I closed my hands tightly and felt the moan leave my chest and float into the quiet of the morning.

"Michael, we leave you where your heart is.

Here where you roamed free with your beloved animals.

A lion among men.

Rest here and know that we love you. Goodbye." My voice petered out.

My hands opened to the wind and the crystals of Michael fell on the bank and rolled into the water. A duiker was drinking thirstily at the waterhole, unconcerned by the human drama being played out in the dappled sunlight.

I stood there with my back to the others. Kelly walked to the Land Rover.

Vusi walked to the water's edge. He held his hands high and I saw him throw the remainder of the crystals far into the water, disturbing the duiker. It picked up its head and swiftly disappeared into the brush.

The roar of the lion was close. Its grunt was distinctive as it sniffed the air. Philemon, with shotgun in hand, motioned us to move towards the vehicle. We were seated and waiting for the next sound when the old lion, with his magnificent mane, stalked out of the bush on the far side of the water. He stood, head held high, looking upwards. He grunted and sniffed. Swishing his tail from side to side he stealthily moved towards the water. We watched spellbound. He walked to the edge of the water, drank deeply and shook his head from side to side. He then turned his back on us and sat down on the soft sand, his tail resting in the water. The awesome sight of that animal with his confidence and his power sent tingles down my spine.

No one spoke, we sat there, lost in our own thoughts. The only person unmoved by the experience was Slabbert. He had leaned back and closed his eyes.

We drove back to the homestead, thinking of our journeys back home. I was dreading my parting with the staff at the homestead. It was so emotional that I cannot find words to describe what happened. I leave that part of my history out of this book.

Kelly drove us home.

I never saw Linda or Slabbert again. I don't know whether they continued their affair. I know she went back to Portugal and divorced Luis. Whether she went back to South Africa or stayed in Portugal, I am still to find out.

CHAPTER THIRTY-ONE

Welcome home!

The next few days passed in a blur of activity. I tried to see as many of my girlfriends as I could and spent some quality time with Kelly. I had managed to get a Qantas flight for the Saturday evening.

Sarah and Amber were overjoyed at the news that I was returning at last. Kelly was not happy. She had been subjected to so much stress over the past months and I kept thinking that it was better for me to be away from her. If I was not living in her apartment, Trevor could not impact on her life.

Trevor had been remarkably quiet over this period. He was heavily involved with his latest lady and they were seen driving in the current addition to the fleet of sports cars – a bright yellow Alfa convertible. He had played his trump card, had carried out his threat and now he was bored. Or so I thought. If only I had known what was in store for me.

He would undoubtedly have known about my plans to return to Australia and I was becoming paranoid that he would do something really vile like harassing me at the airport.

My farewells were made and there were more tears, buckets of them. Kelly and I clung to one another and Jamie, her boyfriend, looked so uncomfortable.

I boarded the jet and strapped myself in, wishing the pilot would take off immediately. I could not wait to get out of South Africa. This was such an alien emotion for me. I was so patriotic and loved my country with deep passion. Every time I left Johannesburg International Airport in the past I would feel the wrench. This time there was only pain and anxiety to get away in the hope that the miles would dilute Trevor's power.

After take-off I took out my notebook. I had some unfinished business. I had to get something off my chest. I started writing.

A Belated Farewell

Michael, of Michael name – never Mike, never Mick.
How much respect you gained from all and sundry.
Your pathway was too short, you had more to give.
Not to learn, you were born wise, but to teach.
You were a teacher, albeit an unwilling one.

Why so shy, why so reclusive – I learned the answers
far too late
Too late to tell you that I understood and felt the pain.
I never had a problem with the aggression, not really.
I could read the anger and the depth of the fear you held.
I did not always understand but sometimes, just
sometimes,
I looked beyond the veil and caught glimpses of the
person
Too hurt and helpless in his pain.
This I believe, manifested in the physical pain.
If only you had placed those sadnesses in that little
calabash
and thrown it into the river.
Remember? I asked you to do it.
You were really angry with me that day – I remember.

The stones on the jetty foretold the future – you knew.
That's why you threw them in the dam.

What made you self-destruct without even trying
to make a new life and walk into the sunset
holding the hand of love and trust.
There could have been someone.
I will, tomorrow or the day after, on Australian soil,
read this letter to you and you will hear how deep my
pain is.
You will know that I never had a friend like you.
I miss you with an ache in my entire body.
This last week, every time I drove past your house, I
wanted to ring the intercom.
Every time I drove past your factory, I looked up at
your window.
Every time I searched through my cell phone directory,
I stopped at your name.
They had deactivated your voicemail.
I could not hear your voice for a last time.
I feel so angry, so cheated.
What the hell were you thinking about when you first
got ill.
You could have had treatment, you could have lived.
Was this your perverse way of getting back at the world.
Forgive my anger, my pain clouds my love.
Stay with me for a while longer.
I feel afraid and very fragile.
Help me in my new life, give me silent strength.
Goodbye my darling, my love stays with you forever.
From the bottom of my heart I thank you for everything
you did for me.
Guiding me through troubled waters and for all the fun
times we shared.

Goodbye my dearest, caring, bravest, best friend.

I folded the letter and put it into my handbag. I would find the right place to read it to Michael. Then I would tear it up and put the past behind me.

At Perth I disembarked for the customary hour's stop and made my way to the Qantas lounge. After freshening my make-up I took my cell phone and dialled the business in Brisbane. The cheerful receptionist, Michelle, whom I had met briefly on my previous trip, answered in her Melbournian accent.

"Hi Michelle, this is Verryn Grant, how are you?"

"I'm good, where are you?"

"Oh, I'm at Perth Airport waiting for my flight to Sydney and then onto Brissy."

"Welcome Home!"

Those words hit me like a ton of bricks. *Welcome home. I was home!*

When Sarah came on the line, I was crying unashamedly.

"Darling, I'm home, isn't that wonderful?"

"Mom, we can't wait to see you. Hurry home." Her voice broke.

My flight into Brisbane landed at 7 p.m. on the Sunday and I rushed into the arms of four pioneering children. The two girls and their partners had started the beginning of their new lives in another country. They looked happy and healthy. They loved Australia.

I had it all, beautiful children, a third share in a business in Brisbane. I was healthy, intelligent and had the energy to create a new life. What a challenge. What blessings from God.

All I needed was some rest and then I would take on the world.

CHAPTER THIRTY-TWO

Painting the fear

I joined the family members in Brisbane in restructuring our business activities. No time for dwelling on the trauma suffered in South Africa. The pace was frenetic and I had very little spare time.

I had left all the legal battles in the hands of the lawyers and advocates in South Africa. My legal fees rose on an hourly basis. I was inundated with faxes to the point that I developed an absolute phobia of my private fax machine at home. I used to dread going home and wading through all the letters and counter claims being issued by Trevor's lawyers. I felt more and more insecure about the efficiency of my own lawyers and knew that they were being slack because I was too far away and could not monitor their progress. My requests for action were always fobbed off with the 'time difference'. This was supposedly the reason for their delays on responding to various issues.

Trevor, in the meantime, had developed renewed vigour for vengeance and he had stepped up his campaign of vindictiveness. His claims were mind-boggling and his threats never ending.

He took to calling me in the middle of my nights. His jeering voice jolting me from my troubled sleep as his threats became more and more irrational.

"I am going to frame you further, Verryn. You are going to go down the drain, Verryn. Don't come back here Verryn. Just sign everything over to me and I'll leave you in peace."

And so it went on and on.

My health deteriorated and I began seeing a therapist. She was amazing and helped me deal with my fax machine phobia. After a number of weekly sessions she recommended that I take a trip into the Outback to get away from the business, the family and the fax machine.

I planned my trip and caught the 'Spirit of the Outback' from Brisbane to Longreach and loved every minute of the trip. I had a sleeper compartment to myself and spent long hours lazily watching the Australian landscapes flying past my window. I had dinner in the dining carriage and was swept away by the friendliness of the Aussie travellers. I slept like a log on the bunk bed with its crisp white linen provided by the cheerful porter. I disembarked in Longreach and absorbed the fragrance and the culture of this world where people enjoyed themselves and lived life to the fullest.

On a day trip, way into the Outback, we left the bus at a tourist spot after driving over miles and miles of rough sand roads. I wandered off on my own. We had one hour to do our own thing before leaving for the next tourist attraction.

I looked for some shade and sat down on a tree stump with a cold bottle of mineral water in my hand. At first I did not notice the man. He was sitting flat on the ground. His face was grimy and his hair wild and unruly. His motley attire could not be identified to that of any particular culture but he looked strange – to me, anyway.

I stared at him and got quite a fright when he raised his hand and beckoned me to join him. Haltingly I moved forward.

"Hi, how are you?' My voice did not portray the confidence I hoped it would. In his strange accent he told me to sit, patting the sand. I sat and waited, my heart speeding up. He began drawing circles in the sand, talking softly. At first I could not make out what he was saying. Suddenly I could master the accent and understood. He wrote letters in the sand, no particular order, all jumbled up – R T V R.

My mind was reeling, he was spelling TREVOR! I knew it. Next to him were some planks of wood. Now I saw that he made his living by doing spur of the moment paintings for the tourists. He took a piece of charcoal and started drawing. In silent fascination I watched this native of Australia draw my face. It was lined with absolute fear and terror– eyes like a hunted deer.

I sat there, stunned beyond words. He handed me the piece of wood and his words will echo in my mind for the rest of my life.

"Missus, you be right. The man won't win. His power gone under earth. You don't give up."

I took out my purse to give him money. He shook his head from side to side. I put it back. I held out my hand wanting to shake his hand. He gave me his right hand and we sat like old friends holding hands. A woman and her husband walking past gave me the strangest look. They hurried on, not wanting to be part of this.

I took my drawing, got up and waved goodbye to my friend and joined the queue for boarding the bus.

Somehow I had a feeling of dread but there was also a feeling of strength welling up in me. I knew that I was going to walk through the fires of hell but I would survive. I got home from my trip to Longreach and waited for the storm.

It came soon after. Trevor had laid his plans very well. His money had triumphed again and again. He wanted to destroy me. He was planning the final countdown.

I took the call on the extension in my bedroom. The jeering voice echoed across the international line. "I've framed you my dear, so tightly you won't escape this one. I am going to have you extradited and you will never see those darling kids of yours again."

I dropped the phone, ran to my study and pulled out the telephone plug. I ran to the lounge, pulled out the plug on the portable phone, ran back to my bedroom and wrenched that plug out of the wall. By now I was crying hysterically.

I woke up on the carpet in my bedroom. I had passed out from sheer terror and exhaustion. The next morning I phoned the girls telling them I was ill. Sarah arrived at my townhouse an hour later. I was in bed unable to get up and incapable of dressing myself. My mind had gone into a secret place, far away from Trevor.

I stayed in bed for a week while Sarah and Amber took turns at nursing me. I slept day and night.

It was a Saturday afternoon. I was in bed reading one of Sarah Henderson's books that Amber had bought for me. Her words were prophetic, "Mom, this Australian woman battled against all the odds and she came out winning. You will too."

Sarah was sitting in the chair next to my bed when the phone rang.

"Hi Kelly, how are you my darling sis!"

Her face froze, and then she yelled, "Tell me the whole story. Start over, go slowly."

Watching her I first felt trepidation at her initial reaction, then I relaxed, the news could not be too bad. She was smiling from ear to ear. "Bye Kells, we'll phone you later. Love you."

Sarah put the phone down, took my book out of my hands, yanked me up and hugged me. She was suffocating me and I wanted to know what was going on.

"You're free Mom, you're FREE!"

"What do you mean, free? Please tell me what's going on!"

"The Troll died last night – he's DEAD!"

Slow realisation crept over me. The nickname for Trevor

had been used from time to time when the girls were frustrated and angry with him.

I lay back on the pillows and Sarah recounted the story told to her by her sister.

Trevor had gone to his favourite Portuguese restaurant in Bedfordview. His latest lady was with him. As he walked out of the restaurant he suffered a massive heart attack and died before the paramedics could get him to the nearby clinic.

"His hate killed him. He thrived on other people's misery. Good riddance to that evil swine." Sarah's expression was cold and angry.

I mulled over what she had just told me. I agreed that his hate had killed him. It had contaminated his body and his soul. I was free. YES!

CHAPTER THIRTY THREE

A new life

A month went by and I regained my emotional strength literally by the minute. I felt like a human being and not like a hunted deer.

I decided to move away from the city. The Sunshine Coast beckoned. The beautiful beaches, the mountain ranges and the friendliness of the people was too much to resist. The girls agreed that I could work flexible hours and we started planning for a branch of the business in Maroochydore.

I started house hunting and every weekend would drive down to Buderim and stay with my friend, Valerie. She would have mountains of newspapers for me to wade through the property for sale sections and she knew a few real estate agents.

Val arranged the appointment that was predestined.

When I walked into the townhouse I knew it was meant for me. The atmosphere was warm and welcoming and the lady selling it exuded sincerity and kindness. It needed a bit of work doing to it but in general it was just what I needed. I paid my deposit and insisted on an early occupation date. I simply had to move in and create my nest.

After signing all the papers, Val and I decided to drive up the range to Montville and have lunch at one of the quaint little restaurants. We sat there enjoying a leisurely lunch of crisp salad and home-made bread, excitedly discussing curtains, paint colours and a new layout for the tiny little garden.

Val looked across the restaurant and gave a wave of

recognition. "Well, well, look who's here! I haven't seen Jonathan for years."

The grey-haired man, dressed in pale slacks and a blue shirt, got up from his table and walked across to us. She introduced Jonathan and he joined us for coffee. We chatted amiably for a while and then ordered second coffees. We were enjoying the relaxation from the whirl of house hunting and it was getting late afternoon.

The colours of the trees in the main road of Montville take on a sheen at dusk. I breathed in the fresh air, enjoying the bond of friendship between my friend and Jonathan. Eventually conversation got around to the personal parts and I discovered that he was a widower, a retired barrister from Brisbane, and now lived in Montville. By the strangest co-incidence, his father was born in South Africa and had the exact same Christian names as my father.

"Have you been into the Outback yet Verryn?" His question jolted my memory back to my trip a couple of months previously.

"Yes, I have, I went to Longreach and then travelled further into Matilda country."

"Did you enjoy it?" His question probed deeper than he would ever know.

"I loved it. I have a friend there. I have to go back soon and visit him."

"A boyfriend?" His question was loaded with teasing and enquiry.

"No, a very special friend. I'll tell you about him one day."

"I'll hold you to that, Verryn, what about dinner tomorrow night?"

My thoughts had drifted back to the wise old man who draws faces. I heard his words, clearly. I had to go and tell him about my new life. Would he already know?

Glossary

Baas	Afrikaans word for boss.
Boma	A circular shelter made out of grass or bamboo found on game farms. Used for entertainment and dining areas. Shelter from wild animals. Usually has a large bonfire going in the entrance.
Braai	Afrikaans word for barbecue.
Bundu bashing	Driving or walking off the beaten track.
Cell phone	Mobile phone.
Duiker	Wild buck.
Gauteng	A Province of South Africa used to be called Transvaal.
Hau	An African exclamation of surprise or questioning.
Highveld	Johannesburg is on the Highveld
Khakibos	Khakibush - a weed.
Kiaat	A type of wood.
Koppies	Small hills.
Lammergeier	Large eagle known for attacking lambs.
Muti	Special medicines or brews made by witchdoctors.
Potjie	Typical African casserole cooked in a three-legged cast iron pot.
Sabona	Greetings in African language.
Sangoma	Witchdoctor. They are highly respected and pass their knowledge on from generation to generation. Some of them are feared due to superstition that they have the power to cast evil spells.

VERRYN'S CALL

Slasto	African version of slate flooring.
Sotho	African tribe.
Tokoloshe	An age-old belief, passed down from generation to generation. This is the name given to a very bad spirit. His form is that of a dwarf or gnome and he is feared greatly. Some ethnic tribes in South Africa raise their beds by placing bricks under the legs. They believe this keeps them safe from the tiny little man who will not reach them whilst they sleep.
Toor	Cast an evil spell.
Tsotsi	African word for thug.
Veld	African landscape.
Xhosa	African tribe.